THOSE
WITHOUT
WINGS

Editing by Julie C. Gilbert

Cover illustration by diandviation

Published by JourneyWorx

More information at gaiusjaugustus.com

THOSE
WITHOUT
WINGS

A Supernatural Fantasy Story

GAIUS J. AUGUSTUS

2025 Second Edition

JourneyWorx

TABLE OF CONTENTS

DEDICATION

To everyone who encouraged me to get my work out
into the world.

INTRODUCTION

Thank you for picking up this novella. I've spent many years with these characters and ideas, and I'm proud to be able to present them to you. Some characters in this work use gender-neutral pronouns. Here is a guide to the usage of a selection of common pronouns.

FEMALE	MALE	GENDER NEUTRAL
She	He	They/Ze/Xe/It
Her	Him	Their/Zir/Xir/It
Hers	His	Theirs/Zirs/Xirs/Its

Examples:

He/She/They/Ze/Xe/It went to the store.
I want to talk to him/her/them/zir/xir/it.
This book is his/hers/theirs/zirs/xirs/its

CONTENT NOTES

This story contains direct or indirect mentions of the following themes. Please ensure you have a care plan in place if any of these items may trigger you. Note that these may contain spoilers. This list may not be comprehensive.

On page death, death of children, manipulative monsters, and suicidal thoughts.

CHAPTER 1

As soon as he opened his eyes, Adams knew he was dead. Like any reasonable person, he was surprised to be opening his eyes at all after such a terminal event. But, like every person who had ever come before him, he wasn't in a reasonable mindset at this moment because, well, he was dead.

This fact wasn't betrayed by the white expanse that stretched indefinitely in every direction, bright yet not glaring. It wasn't the strange awareness overcoming him, telling him things he'd never imagined possible. He just knew. He looked himself over, trying to find something strange about his existence. Everything was fine. He felt fine. He was fine. Except, of course, that he was—surprise, surprise—dead, deceased, and definitely, dearly departed.

He almost had time to wonder where he was when, abruptly, a strong guilt rushed through him. Every lie, every wrong, every minuscule regret pounded on his mind.

1

He had not been an evil man. In fact, as humans go, he was among the best. He was born to a well-to-do family, was left a sizable inheritance, and used that money to support a sister, to start several charitable organizations, and to give himself enough time to volunteer frequently.

Even so, like almost every person before him, he had made mistakes. There were things in his life he felt guilty for. Not all of these regrets were rational, but very few have dared to propose that the afterlife was a rational place.

His most profound regret dealt with the accident that had killed him. Just the reminder brought tears to his eyes. His chest hurt, and his throat felt tight. As his legs weakened, he dropped to his knees, sobbing uncontrollably with the agony of emotional pain.

A deep, slow voice came from behind him. "Hello, Brother."

He could barely force himself to face the old man who had just appeared. The man was large, both tall and wide, and looked joyful yet tired. He wore a long robe, mostly white but with silver embroidery around the hems, and a cloth draped over his shoulders. Had Adams not been wallowing in misery, he might have described the man's vibe as "a bit too comfortable."

Instead, when he opened his mouth to speak, only a cry came out. The grief overtaking him shook him to his core. He fought to control it, to push back this guilt and the intrusive thoughts that made him want to stop existing all together.

"Take your time."

Another nugget of knowledge came to Adams: this man was an angel. This wasn't at all what Adams would have expected in an angel, had he ever expected to meet one at all. The angel seemed too normal, like any other large, old man wearing heavenly robes. However, Adams knew it was true, and in that same moment, he knew he had to make the ultimate decision: what to do with himself in this after-living life.

"I don't know," Adams cried. "It's too difficult."

How could he make such a decision so quickly? Every fiber of his shame told him to end it, to combine with all the energy of the universe, where he would feel no guilt, nothing at all. Yet it seemed so final, and he couldn't bring himself to say it.

"There's no need to rush to a decision. Let's just talk. My name is Stiggens."

Stiggens took his time when he spoke, as if savoring every word that slipped from his lips. His deportment was calm as a gentle breeze, and his whole body expanded and contracted as he took slow, deep breaths. Adams realized that he was breathing as well, and Stiggens noticed his surprise right away.

"Breath," Stiggens said. "Breath is something we all have within us. We do not need it, yet we continue to use it. It allows us to feel closer to Midrealm."

Midrealm. Adams suddenly knew this, too. It was the name for the reality he had once occupied, a reality of physical matter and linear time. The reality where everyone he'd ever known was born, grew old, and died. It was a universe full of incredible, ancient wonders and modern marvels, of amazing, compassionate heroes and cruel,

3

pathetic villains. Of course, there was also everything in between, as well. The complexity of Midrealm terrified him, but Adams was too busy feeling sorry for himself to realize.

The angels lived on one level of a different reality, Highrealm, where they existed as energy yet expressed pseudo-physical representations of themselves in a pseudo-physical environment. They chose to do this in part because it prevented a lot of confusion, but also because it was fun. Adams could almost see Highrealm in his mind. Even as he imagined it, his expectations were altering the realm. To live in Highrealm was to experience a dynamic existence formed by the collective consciousness of all who occupied it. The dreams and imaginations of every angel were crafted into a welcoming space that was ever-changing.

Adams wondered what he could achieve there: the lives he could change and the feats he could accomplish. Yet he struggled to convince himself that he deserved to occupy the same space as angels such as the one standing in front of him. As the weight of his guilt pushed down on him, he fought against it, to regain his composure, and to stand.

Ever so slowly, he did. Adams was nothing if not persistent. Or was it stubborn? Either way, he pushed himself to his feet and met the angel's gaze.

This level of intensity was as unnecessary as it was rare. Ancient angels such as Stiggens aren't easily impressed, but Adams had always been an overachiever.

"Many cannot handle their guilt," Stiggens remarked. "They fall to the floor unable to rise, unable to speak, unable to bear it, no matter how long they try. Of those, some wish to return to Midrealm. They wish to somehow right their wrongs, to be purged of their knowledge of all that is, and to start anew."

"They're reborn?" Adams asked.

"Yes. New bodies, new lives, new memories, new experiences." Stiggens laughed a little to himself. "They often make the same mistakes, but that's the way things are, and it brings them comfort."

He paused for a long while. His silence made Adams wonder if he was thinking about something, but then he suddenly began again.

"Others who cannot bear the guilt join with the Source. Do you understand the Source yet?"

Though Adams was standing now, his head was still reeling. "It's energy, the final destination of all energy in the universe."

Stiggens nodded his head gently, as if moving too quickly would cause him to fall. Given that they were surrounded by an endless sea of white, who knew how far he could roll.

Adams continued, "The Source exists in another level of Highrealm, closer to where the immortals live."

"Now, now. We are also immortals, in a way. We exist for as long as we see fit. After a time, most angels choose to move on to the Source or be reborn. Those that exist closer to the Source are not so different, yet they hold more knowledge of the universe and its interconnection with time."

"What should I do?" Adams asked.

The coherence of thought he was used to was returning to him—much faster than was typical, although Adams had no knowledge of this fact. Every second was a battle to maintain it, and he was wrapped up in the fight.

"I can't decide for you," Stiggens said. "There are many options available to you. You know them just as well as I, isn't that correct?"

Adams sighed. "I can become an angel. Is that really true?"

"Of course, Brother. It's your choice to make. Your guilt will follow you there and will stay with you. But there are rare souls who choose to become angels."

Most of the newly dead took their time making this decision, sometimes the equivalent of decades. Adams wasn't the type of man to make decisions lightly, and in different circumstances, he may have needed at least a few minutes.

However, unlike any other before him, a disembodied whisper—clear yet silent—snuck into Adams's ear. It called on him to make a decision as if it was as clear as day. The guilt still hung over him, threatening to drag him into its clutches at any moment. He struggled to hold onto his footing and not be overcome with grief. He couldn't help but wonder if it was even possible to exist with such a feeling always upon him.

Yet he knew—as he knew he was dead and as he knew Stiggens was an angel—that his place was in the Realm of the Angels. He knew he still had work to do.

Adams was given time to settle into his new after-life life. He was given living quarters, which seemed more like a pocket of space within the Realm. These quarters conformed to his needs and wants, yet it was practically empty. It had developed simple architecture like the apartment he had been living in, meaning it had four walls, a ceiling, and a floor. It was cozy enough, but lonely.

He couldn't stand being there for long periods of time and so wandered around, trying to find excuses to be busy. He'd been told there were many options for work. At some point, he would have to choose something, and while he had tried to learn about different choices, none of the information seemed to stick.

His thoughts were consumed by his ten-year-old niece, Illeina, who had been in the same accident that killed him. She wasn't in this realm; he could sense that. He assumed she had joined with the Source. He often asked himself whether he should have done the same. Stiggens had told him that he could change his mind. However, it didn't seem right, not yet.

Illeina had just barcly turned ten when they died. For her birthday, he had organized a small party for her, renting a gazebo at a public park near where he lived. She loved that park, especially climbing in the network of treehouses that the neighborhood community association had assembled. Adams always ended up climbing after her, bumping his head on doorways and making her laugh at his suffering. At her birthday, she kept glancing at the treehouses, but diligently thanked everyone for coming and for her presents.

His sister had come over to him as everyone ate cake and hugged him tightly. "Thank you again," she'd said.

He smiled and squeezed her as he replied. "Of course. She's my only niece. I have to spoil her."

"Work keeps you busy, but you always make time for her."

"I know she has a big family on your husband's side and several cousins nearby to play with. But she means a lot to me. I probably won't have kids anytime soon."

She had laughed at him, tossing him back and forth in her continuing hug. "You'll meet someone someday and maybe even have a daughter of your own. You are the most amazing person I know, after all."

It gnawed at him thinking of how much hope she had for her brother, and now here he was, wallowing in guilt while he was supposed to be making a difference. He couldn't imagine how heartbroken she must be. Their parents had died years earlier, and they had no other family left. Now she had lost all that was left: her brother and child.

As he tried to push the thoughts from his mind, he found a bench on a balcony overlooking what appeared to be a forest. He had been told that it was not a forest at all; the trees were not trees, but as much created by the community as everything else. Adams didn't care what they said. It looked like a forest to him, and it didn't feel artificial at all.

Its scent was familiar to him. He recognized it from the hardwood forest just beyond the Midrealm city he had lived in. He took Illeina there a few times each summer to camp. Illeina adored exploring the outdoors, and it was often hard for him to keep her on the trails. Camping was a different story, and she complained every year about the small, old tent they shared. He had promised her they would go the next summer and buy a new tent together.

Buying that tent for her seemed like such a simple request now, and he wondered how many more forests he could have shown her had he bought one sooner. And he wondered, were there any forests on Earth that compared to this one?

This forest in the Realm of the Angels was a training ground, where angels spent a large portion of their time when they first arrived. He would train here at some point, once he had chosen what he wanted to do. When he had asked Stiggens what kind of training there would be, Stiggens just smiled in his strange way and told Adams there was plenty of time.

The balcony sat close to the top of the nearby trees, while other trees towered far above him. Below, he could hear the voices of angels. There was a loud boom, and then laughter.

Training with explosives? Was that possible? Maybe it was some kind of competition. He reached his neck out and leaned forward to see, but the foliage was too thick.

So, he sat back and sighed, looking up into the artificial blueness of the sky. Artificial white puffs of clouds dotted the expanse. It all looked and felt so real that he wished they were anything else. He wished this was all a dream so he could tell himself he might one day wake up.

"Hello," a voice said from behind Adams and his lonely bench.

He'd been totally zoned out for, well, he didn't know how long. He looked back to put a kind face to the voice and returned the greeting.

"You're still feeling the guilt, aren't you?" ze said.

Adams was taken aback. The other angels he had met were distant, in order to give him adequate time to process his guilt, or that's what Stiggens told him. Yet this angel had no qualms with jumping into a heavy topic right away.

"How can you tell?" he asked zir.

"You're sulking. Almost any time I see someone sulking, they're still weighed down." Ze sat down next to him. "My name is Casey."

"I go by Adams, my family name."

"It's nice to meet you, Adams. Would you prefer I leave you to your sulking?"

Adams sighed and shook his head.

"So, what's on your mind?" Casey asked.

Casey was different from the other angels he had met so far. Ze seemed full of life, yet boldly curious. His understanding was that asking a newcomer this kind of question was rare. Others seemed cautiously friendly, as if speaking about it would bring their own guilt to the surface. Casey had no such inhibition, and it was refreshing.

"Besides everything?" he replied, and he felt calmed when Casey laughed. "I've actually been thinking about my niece, Illeina."

"You were close?"

"Very close. I loved her as if she was my own." Adams sighed. "We both died in a motorcycle accident."

"Was she a child?"

He nodded and replied, "She was ten years old." A small glimmer of pride bubbled up when he didn't immediately start crying again.

"It's good that she had someone in her life who loved her, but of course, it's always sad when a child dies."

Adams put his head in his hands, that overwhelmed feeling starting to creep up from his stomach into his chest. So much for that sense of pride.

"There were people who loved you, too, Adams," Casey continued. "They are in pain, just as you are. You still share that bond. But you can't fault yourself for something that may have been fated."

"I'm not sure I believe in fate."

"Not everything that happens is fate," Casey explained. "But a very small proportion of events **are** fated. There are things in this universe that we **know** will occur. There are prophecies that come and go and fork."

"Fork?" Adams asked, lifting his head to meet zirs. "What does that mean?"

"Well, prophecy isn't always as straightforward as 'this person will create that outcome.' Sometimes, the way things occur can shape and mold the prophecy, even though the overall form of the prophecy remains the same." Casey was waving zir hands around as if it made zir explanation make sense.

It did not.

"Is there some prophecy about my niece?" Adams asked.

"I don't know. I'm just saying that some things are fated, and if her death was, nothing you could have done would have changed that."

This did not soothe Adams at all. In fact, this just made him feel worse. Maybe he should have just told zir to give him some space.

"Thanks for trying," was all he could bring himself to say.

"I work in the Archive," Casey said, "so I read and follow the prophecies closely. It gives me a unique perspective on things, I guess. I didn't mean to upset you."

Ze stood to leave, but Adams took a deep breath.

"It's nice to have someone to talk to," he said. "Let's just talk about something else."

Casey was cautious and hesitated for a long while. Adams watched as ze looked around, as if looking for another reason to leave, before sitting back down. Although this stretched out longer than the typical pause, it somehow didn't feel awkward. Casey must be overflowing with charisma, Adams decided.

He was reminded of a time when Illeina was very small, and although she wasn't loud, she was opinionated. She often would go up to people and ask them questions. His sister would be so embarrassed when Illeina did this, but Adams thought it was amazing. Almost everyone Illeina spoke to left the encounter with a genuine smile on their face.

Even so, one day while her mother was at the doctor, Illeina found her way to a patient's room. Adams had tried to catch up to her, but couldn't stop her before she went into the room and up to the woman sitting within.

Illeina asked the woman if she was okay, and the woman responded that her husband had just died. Illeina asked what that meant, and the woman told her she would never see her husband again. Illeina had cried like he'd never seen before. She was inconsolable, even after Adams took her from the room and coddled her outside. For a month, Illeina avoided strangers, and then suddenly, she was back to asking questions again as if nothing had ever happened.

Something about Casey seemed to spark the same pride he had felt the first time Illeina was back to questioning. It was a strength about her that he had always appreciated, to be so resilient after a bad experience. He had often questioned whether all children showed such resilience, but that didn't make it any less remarkable to him.

He sat for a long time with Casey, asking questions about the Realm. It felt good to be interacting with another person, and it was almost enough for him to believe he could bear this existence.

Almost.

CHAPTER 2

Adams found it a comfort to spend time with Casey, and he began doing so often. He understood that his guilt would weigh on him for all eternity, but he was slowly accepting that and moving forward. Casey often invited Adams to attend social events, and soon, he was a quite popular — if somewhat broody — angel.

Casey sometimes asked Adams if he was aware of how everyone seemed drawn to him. Ze explained that while everyone got along well for the most part in the Realm of the Angels, ze had never seen anyone quite as likable. It may have been his subtle but strong charm, but it was more likely his willingness to dance despite his lack of skill.

When other angels invited Adams to parties and gatherings, he always made sure to include Casey. He noticed that angels were awkward around zir, but when he asked about it, his concern was brushed off. In truth, everyone was kind to them both, yet Adams couldn't help but wonder if there was something he was missing about zir.

Among the great number of people he met were people from other worlds. In life, Adams had wondered if life existed beyond Earth, but there had been no use thinking too hard about it because the truth wasn't known. The great variety of species he met as an angel was astounding, and it took getting used to. Even so, he could always understand them, as if they all spoke a universal language, or perhaps they all were able to understand the disparate languages that existed in the universe. Adams had never had a knack for learning foreign languages, so he relished the opportunities to compare cultural ideology, music, and stories.

It was all a welcome distraction.

There came a day when Stiggens came to visit him. He knew without looking that the knock was Stiggens, as the door was connected to him—just as everything in his quarters was. After he invited Stiggens in, the older angel slowly eased into the room. Adams offered him a seat and waited while the man slowly considered his options and finally sat onto a sofa in the middle of the room.

"It's time for you to choose your role," the man said when Adams asked why he was visiting.

"I see. I suppose you're right."

"Have you thought about what you'd like to do? I've heard that you've been asking others about their duties. I'm impressed by the speed of your acceptance, Brother, and I look forward to your future here."

"Truthfully, sir—" Adams started.

"Have they not explained to you?" Stiggens interrupted in his own slow manner. "There is no true hierarchy here. We are all brothers and sisters and friends."

Adams had assumed the brother, sister language was because no one wanted to learn everyone else's name. Obviously, it held more meaning than that.

Stiggens shifted in his seat. "Friend Casey told me ze has accompanied you to many activities. Perhaps you're interested in working in the Archive with zir."

"I don't think that kind of thing is right for me," Adams confessed. "I'd rather work with people."

"Well, as you know, there are several opportunities for that. You can work with intake to help the newly deceased accept their deaths and choose their next path."

"That's what you do, isn't it, Stiggens?"

"No, Brother. You were a special case."

Adams raised an eyebrow and cocked his head to the side with curiosity, so Stiggens continued.

"Every once in a while, an immortal from closer to the Source communicates a particular interest in an individual. It isn't so much that they favor you, more so that they see some future for you. Often, instead of sharing any details, an individual is chosen by the immortal to do intake for this newly deceased person."

"I . . . I'm honored," Adams stuttered.

Stiggens let out a slow, even laugh.

Adams grimaced. "Should I not be?"

"Oh, no," Stiggens said. "Feel free to be honored. I'm merely amused by the concept."

"Why?"

17

"As I've mentioned, Brother, there are no true hierarchies here. The hierarchy that exists is purely in the minds of those who live here, whose lives were often driven by societal hierarchies, and who feel it necessary to function as part of our society. As such, an immortal cannot honor us as they are not above us."

If Adams hadn't known any better, he would have thought the man was patronizing him. But that was more Casey's style.

Stiggens dipped into another of his bouts of silence, as if he forgot what he was going to say.

Just as Adams opened his mouth to respond, Stiggens continued. "I often think that when an immortal requests a particular angel to welcome a soul, they do so with balance in mind. The immortals rarely interfere with the affairs of Midrealm, but we in the Realm of the Angels do. I am sure they see patterns we do not, and seek balance in the universe in things we do not yet understand.

"There are individuals who have joined with the Source as a recommendation of an immortal. There are others who have become a part of our realm. We all fulfill our roles here, but I suppose sometimes there is a need to fill a certain position, and perhaps that is why a certain person becomes of interest."

"What's in store for me, then?" Adams asked.

"The immortals never share their plans with us. Not me, at least. You'll learn all about this once you begin your training." He closed his eyes and shook his head. "I've gone off on a tangent. My apologies."

18

"That's right. We were discussing options for roles."

"Perhaps you are more suited to be a guardian. You'll be assigned individuals who you can identify with, and then you'll help them throughout their lives. Would that interest you?"

"Maybe," Adams said, putting a hand to his chin as he considered it. "Is there anything where I can go to Midrealm? Perhaps even see my family?"

"Ah," Stiggens said with a knowing — and possibly patronizing — grin. "Transference to Midrealm is restricted to a particular area of our realm. It is used for angels who do tasks there, such as Messengers and Mourners. You've heard of those?"

Adams tilted his head side to side. "Briefly."

"Messengers carry verbal or emotional messages between angels in Midrealm and here, as well as from angels to those who still live. Mourners stay with families of the deceased and ease their emotional burden."

"And would I be able to see my family?"

"Messengers often tell me they are able to take a little time to observe the living while in Midrealm. Perhaps that would be a viable option for you." Stiggens spoke slowly, and Adams's excitement built as he spoke.

He wanted to shout out his agreement, but instead waited impatiently for the man to finish before blurting out an excited request. "Please allow me to be a Messenger."

Stiggens let out another slow laugh. With a low groan, he pushed himself off the sofa and returned to his feet.

"I am not a trainer. However, I've been asked to carry out your training as well. We will begin tomorrow. I will call for you to meet me in the Northern Training Grounds."

"I look forward to it," Adams replied.

He held the door as Stiggens made his way through.

Before Adams closed it, he asked, "Stiggens, if you aren't assigned to intake and you aren't a trainer . . . well, then what is your job?"

"I'm a member of the High Council," he replied plainly before turning and going on his way.

Adams was taken aback. The High Council was the governing body of the angels. They assessed the validity of the current angelic laws, The Celestial Code, decided punishments when necessary, and handled requests and disputes when they arose.

For example, Casey had told Adams that recently several family members had each requested to be guardian for their descendants. They hoped an audience with the High Council would determine who was the best fit. The High Council had divided up their descendants based on their needs and allowed a small amount of overlap in jurisdiction.

Adams elation was so profound that he immediately sought Casey out. When he asked how the High Council was chosen, Casey explained that they were some of the oldest and most experienced angels, and that they existed closer to the true energy form of Highrealm than any of the other angels. Adams couldn't help feeling honored to have a member of the High Council assigned to train him. With much difficulty, he tried to contain his excitement and remember that there was no hierarchy in the Realm of the Angels. The thought enthralled him, despite his best efforts.

He asked zir as many questions as he could muster about the High Council, about Stiggens, and about training. Casey seemed to find humor in his curiosity and enthusiasm, much as Stiggens had, except ze wasn't afraid to laugh in his face.

"I'm excited for you, too," Casey patronized him.

"When I was alive, I was part of an international consortium," Adams said. "We worked toward policies that we hoped would prevent wars and bring global peace. It constantly felt like it was falling apart. During the last year of my life, I felt like it was over, and that our last chance was gone. I really believed that the next generation would grow up in a dystopian world that didn't care about its impact on the planet, much less future generations. But this . . . this is another chance for me. I can make a difference. I can feel it."

"Well, there's some reason for it," Casey said. "And it seems pretty unlikely that a High Council member would be assigned to train you just for balance."

Adams couldn't help but hug Casey for understanding—or pretending to understand—what he was feeling. Ze patted his back gently and laughed again. Undeterred, only moments passed before Adams started asking more questions.

Adams slept on a regular schedule, despite never feeling tired and despite day and night not existing in Highrealm. It just seemed right to lie down, close his eyes, and imagine what lay before him. On this particular day, his mind drifted to Casey's thoughts about prophecy. He wondered if there was some prophecy about him.

He imagined himself changing the world. Perhaps inspiring a new reign of peaceful conversations between nations, or sparking a widespread belief in the human family as one unit. Instead, maybe he would change the system of the angels somehow. Or it could be that he would provide relief for a living person who would do all the wonderful things he never could.

Was he thinking too small? Could it be that he changed the very state of being in the universe?

His dreams of grandeur were interrupted by Stiggens requesting his presence at the Northern Training Grounds. He quickly looked himself over and ran a comb through his hair before jogging to the false forest of the training grounds.

The entrance was quite grand, flanked by two trees so enormous that he couldn't comprehend their height. They were wider than he was tall, and a strange golden red. The first branches began at thrice his height and stretched their thick branches to entangle together. The bark's pattern reminded him of an esoteric art piece he had seen once, where thousands of lines had made their way in intricate patterns down the canvas, creating all shapes and sizes of polygons. Walking under these trees, Adams was in awe of how small he felt, even though he was an angel, which he still thought was very neat.

Stiggens was waiting a short walk within, and when Adams told him that he had rushed there, Stiggens smiled.

"As you know, there was no reason to hurry," he said in his usual slow way.

"I know you've said that time is meaningless here, but I don't understand."

Stiggens grinned. "There is nothing more to say. Time is relative, for humans in Midrealm and for us here. In the angelic realm, our lack of a physical reality makes it even more subjective. You'll come to understand this the longer you're here."

Adams's head was reeling already, and he knew they hadn't even begun. Still, he was eager to get started. They made their way to a small clearing, where Stiggens had Adams sit at the center. He formed a small ball of energy while telling Adams to hold it gently.

"Just try to keep it from dissipating," Stiggens said as if it was the simplest thing in the world.

It was not simple. In fact, no matter how hard Adams tried, it disappeared just as it hit his hands.

"What am I doing wrong?" Adams asked.

"You're thinking too hard about it," Stiggens replied. "Just let it happen, like catching a raindrop."

Adams wanted to learn this, probably more than he'd ever wanted to learn anything. Even though he'd enjoyed learning things in life, he'd never wanted it this much. A silent whisper spurred him onward, and he couldn't articulate why he needed to listen.

Much later, Adams would find amusement in how desperate he'd been at learning the most minor of skills, which every angel learned. But at this moment, nothing seemed more essential than what he was failing at over and over. He grew more frustrated, which Stiggens ignored at first, but finally paused.

"I'm ready!" Adams exclaimed when he realized the angel wasn't creating another ball of energy.

"Yes, I know," Stiggens replied. "I'm afraid that I'm a little tired. Perhaps we'll take a rest."

It was a lie, and Adams should have known that. But he allowed himself to indulge in the deception because it was done as a gesture of kindness. And yes, angels can lie, and they do quite often. This has led to many problems, some which might better be classified as disasters.

"I'm sorry," Adams replied. "Of course. Please rest."

Stiggens grunted as he lowered himself to the ground next to Adams. He took one of his slow, deep breaths.

"When I first arrived here," Stiggens said, "it felt like a year before I could stand with my guilt. There were many things that never bothered me until I died. The weight of it all was incredible, as you know. There were some days that I thought of giving up and taking another course of action. I often thought it was impossible to exist with the guilt of all I'd done."

He placed his hands on his knees and took a few— yes slow—deep breaths before continuing.

"Then one day, I wondered what this realm looked like, and I peered out of my room. I saw something out of a fairy tale. I couldn't leave, only stare. An older angel was walking by and called out to me. She smiled and told me she had been looking forward to meeting me, as she had been a guardian to my family for many years. I didn't understand what that meant, but I took a step out to thank her.

"My world changed. I hadn't realized all the knowledge that had been imparted onto me, and I suddenly had so many questions." He smiled at the memory. "Sometimes, it just takes a small push . . ."

He formed a ball in his hands, threw it in the air, and caught it.

"I don't understand," Adams replied.

"That's alright, Brother." Stiggens chuckled. He threw the ball up and down a few more times.

Adams sighed, thinking of the remarkable future he had imagined for himself. He couldn't even do this simple thing, so how could he be special? Everything Stiggens said was true. He was just a balance, a gap that needed to be filled. All he could hope to accomplish was to be the best angel he could.

Just as he was about to respond to Stiggens' story, the old angel suddenly threw the ball too high. Adams jumped in alarm as it drifted in the wind and plummeted toward the ground. Instinctively, he leaned far and fell to the ground with his arms outstretched, catching the ball. He looked at it, glowing so brightly that he could feel warmth coming from it, and smiled.

"I see we've completed our work for today," Stiggens said.

"What? But I just got it. We should do more," Adams argued.

Stiggens laughed, round body jiggling in jubilant undulations. "There is plenty of time, Brother, and this is just the first step of many. Reflect on it."

Adams was in the middle of arguing another point while helping Stiggens to his feet when Casey's voice called out from behind him. He turned to see his friend. He tried to explain how Stiggens was underestimating him, to which Casey laughed.

Ze put an arm around his shoulders. "I have a better idea. I hear you're going to become a Messenger. And I just happen to know that a new batch of Messenger recruits is holding their training at this very moment. I thought you'd like to go watch for a while." Ze smiled at Stiggens. "If your trainer wouldn't mind."

"Of course not, Friend. We are done for today," Stiggens said.

Before Adams could argue, Stiggens turned and left. It was the fastest thing Adams had ever seen Stiggens do.

"Fine," Adams grunted.

As soon as they caught sight of the training, Casey noticed a change in Adams's demeanor. The angels were molding colored energy, pushing and pulling it between them. Their trainer held an orb at the center of the group, and the color drifted out of it in discrete yet wispy clouds. The shape of the clouds transformed into objects as they approached the angels: a dog, a tree, a child.

"What's happening?" Adams asked.

"You know what Messengers do, don't you?" Casey asked.

"Uh . . . deliver messages?"

Ze shot him a disbelieving look, then chuckled. "Well, yes, but how?"

Ze let Adams think for a moment before answering zir own question.

"The messages often have an oral component, but words rarely convey the full meaning of a message. If I tell you that I believe in you, that's a message, but if I can convey my feelings of pride and my desire for you to take responsibility . . . well, that's much more powerful. And accurate, to boot. If I can show you what I see for your future, that visualization gives it even more power."

"So that orange light," Adams started, unsure of exactly how to continue the question.

"It's a visualization of a message," Casey replied. "Early on, the trainer colors the emotional energy so that students can get used to the sensations associated with the emotion. The students are taking messages of a certain kind and translating images embedded in them. They start off simple, with concrete things like objects. But once they master that, they'll learn to create imagery and fill it with the deep emotion that lies within a message."

"Can they create visualizations outside of the training grounds, then?"

"If they become powerful enough, yes. But most can't. Most messages are transmitted through the recipient's dreams, when they are most receptive." Casey seemed perpetually amused at Adams's overwhelming excitement, and this moment wasn't any exception. "You're way too excited to just be a Messenger."

"I'm going to visit my family," Adams said plainly. "I'm going to apologize to them and help them, if I can."

"Apologize?"

Adams would say no more, but he was suddenly very serious. He was certainly determined to see his family again, and although he had never disclosed the circumstances of his and his niece's deaths, Casey rightfully believed a huge part of Adams's guilt must lie there.

Adams doubled his efforts thereafter. All concepts of time were lost to him as he plunged into the manipulation of energy. As he improved, he realized he could feel everything around him. A bench was no longer a bench, but instead a collection of energy that manifested as a bench. The wood texture felt genuine, the scent smelled authentic, but the energetics were wrong. It wasn't a bench at all. When he explained this to Stiggens, the old angel reminded him that the aesthetics of the Realm of the Angels were highly subjective.

When not training, Adams became increasingly interested in how the Realm was interpreted. To him, the sun rose in a perceived east and set in a perceived west. It was yellow in the sky, except at the red- and purple-tinged perceptions of dawn and dusk. Clouds dusted the sky in differing patterns, and there was even an occasional pleasant shower of rain accompanied by comforting rumbles of thunder. The floors were a white marble, and covered pathways led to each door. Large columns were spaced at regular intervals, also made of marble. The wooden benches scattered around the Realm were stained a rich reddish-brown, but were ornamented with gold. There were many areas that overlooked atria, some which held more hallways of doors, but others that overlooked flowing rivers and rippling ponds. The railings were a clear glass that never smudged, always staying crystal clear.

When he asked Casey how ze perceived the Realm, ze replied, "It usually looks like night to me."

"Night? Why night?"

"I've always loved the night," ze replied with a shrug.

Adams looked around him. It was noon to him, the middle of the day. "So right now, it's night?"

"Yes." Casey laughed. "I can point out constellations to you, or the moon, if you'd like."

"But if it's always dark, how can you see?"

"I wish to see," Casey said. "So, I see clearly."

Adams didn't quite understand, so he instead moved on. "What about the ground?"

"It looks like grass to me. And what you call columns, I see as tree trunks. Of course, some things are the same. The loggias are still open, overlooking lower levels. And doors to an angel's quarters will always look like the door the owner wishes it to be. Benches and railings are in the same locations. But it doesn't matter if they're wood or plastic or diamond."

Adams left this conversation appalled and amazed in equal measure. He spent the two days after meditating, focusing extensively on changing his perception of the Realm. And it didn't take long for him to create a world where the sun stayed out longer and where two moons hung low in the sky, which he named after his sister and niece.

Unlike most others, he began his Messenger training while also continuing his work with Stiggens. It went by quickly for him, and he enthusiastically awaited its completion.

As he learned to manipulate messages, he slowly and carefully crafted his own. He focused the emotion on the intense love he felt for his sister and his sadness at leaving her while also balancing his pride in the work he was going to do—someday—as an angel. He created a visualization of playing with her as children, laughing excitedly. Illeina joined them, content and happy. He and Illeina both had angel wings, and they felt warm and soft when they brushed against skin. They hugged, and his sister kissed them both over and over on their cheeks and foreheads and noses. It was joyful.

On the day of his first mission, he ate lunch with Casey, which is also something angels do, not because they have to, but because it brings them comfort. Ze was overly interested in the first message he would be sending.

"I'm confused. Can you explain it again?"

"It's simple," Adams said. "The message is from a Guardian to someone who interacts with one of their descendants. The woman is in love with the Guardian's descendant but has been afraid to speak to him about it. She wants to encourage the woman to be brave and to see where the relationship will lead."

"That doesn't sound so simple to me," Casey huffed, propping zir head on zir hands.

"I spoke with the Guardian for a while and crafted the message with her. She really liked it."

Casey's lip curled into a wry grin. "I just love how you take things too far. You could have just taken the message, but no. You have to work for that extra credit."

Adams couldn't deny it, so he just shrugged in response.

When he was called to deliver the message, his supervisor went over the protocols with him. He showed the supervisor what he had created with the Guardian. The supervisor was so moved that his eyes teared up, and he called another supervisor to show her as well. Finally, after showcasing the work to other Messengers—and staying humble as everyone marveled at his creation—they sent Adams on his way. He was confident, in the perfect mood to deliver his own message.

Once he transferred to Midrealm, he was able to move more freely. He shifted about as energy and traveled more quickly than he had thought possible. It felt as if he was being pulled along by a raging river, yet he was able to fully control his movements. Angels weren't allowed to use their energy in this way in the Realm of the

Angels, as it was easily sensed by others and could be-come bothersome. However, because most inhabitants of Midrealm couldn't sense the energy of an angel, it was no problem to push himself to his limits.

He reached his target's home almost instanta-neously—humble brag—and the delivery of the Guardian's message went flawlessly. The woman inter-acted with the dream just as he planned, even though he had accounted for many variations just in case. Her dream self seemed confident and empowered.

As he turned to leave, however, he noticed she had a large alarm clock on her nightstand. A calendar sat next to it, and when he leaned in, he saw that she had put an "X" for each day that had passed. She also listed tasks for the day on the calendar and checked them off as they were completed. And as he bent down to look at the date in disbelief, he gasped at its confirmation.

It had been over nine months since his death. He tried to recall precisely how much time had gone by, but it all ran together. And he reminded himself that it could have felt like a day and that would mean nothing, since time could pass so differently between Midrealm and the Realm of the Angels.

That was a big oops.

Within minutes, he was at the home his sister shared with her husband and mother-in-law. He was sur-prised to find that the couple was awake. He had hoped they would be asleep, since it would be easier to give the message that way.

"She may never wake up," her husband said. "We may need to accept that."

"I don't want to," his sister cried.

"You've been avoiding this far too long, Amanda. We have to talk about this."

Adams was appalled. Had his brother-in-law's mother become ill? Perhaps she was in some medical treatment and not doing well. It brought tears to his eyes. Surely, his sister had been through enough. Did she really need another loss so soon after losing her brother and daughter?

"I said no," Amanda snapped.

Her husband moved to sit next to her and pulled her close.

"I wish my brother was here," she admitted.

"It's his fault we're in this situation," her husband said.

"How can you still hold a grudge against a dead man? I thought you'd moved past this."

"I'm sorry. I know. It's just, whenever we go to the hospital and see her lying there . . ." He choked up and couldn't continue.

A lump grew in Adams's throat as they spoke, realization washing over him.

"I just can't let her go," Amanda said. "She's my little girl."

The tears Adams had been holding back broke through, and he rushed to wipe them away, as if doing so would change what he was hearing.

"Illeina has been lying there for almost a year," her husband said. "The doctors say she may not even be okay if she wakes up."

"I don't care. She might be fine." She shook her head. "Let's talk about this later. I can't think about it right now." It was too late. She broke down crying, barely able to get the words out.

Her husband pulled her close and gently rocked her.

Adams couldn't breathe, couldn't move, couldn't think.

Illeina was alive.

CHAPTER 3

Adams rushed toward the nearest transport point. He still couldn't believe what he had heard. Illeina had been in a coma since he died, meaning she was still alive. He had the audacity to smile, to try to make a new life in the angelic realm, even to dance—albeit poorly—all while she remained in a hospital struggling to stay alive.

How could he not have checked? Why did he assume she was dead? All this time, she'd been lying there, and he'd done nothing to help her. There must be something he could do. Surely, he could help the family he left behind.

Stiggens would help him. He was certain the ancient angel would have answers for all his questions.

When he transported into the Realm of the Angels, those that had seen the Guardian's message bombarded him with questions and support. Brushing them off with a polite word, he telepathically called for Stiggens to expect him. When he arrived at Stiggens door, his mentor was waiting.

Adams found himself artificially out of breath, so Stiggens asked him what was wrong.

"Illeina is alive," Adams finally said.

"Yes," Stiggens replied.

Adams faltered. "Wait. You knew?"

"Of course. It is my job as your mentor to understand your situation." His words were as slow and kind as ever, as if this was a normal conversation.

"Then why didn't you tell me?"

"There is nothing you can do now," Stiggens said. "She's alive. You are no longer. Telling you without you asking would have been counter to all the progress you've made. Do you disagree?"

Of course, Adams couldn't disagree. Had he known, he likely would have been consumed by it. He couldn't have focused on training. Perhaps he would have tried to transport down to her, not knowing what he was doing or any way of helping her. Perhaps he would have lingered there forever.

"Is her fate sealed?" he asked.

"I don't know."

"What's it like being in a coma?"

"I don't know," Stiggens repeated.

"Where is her soul?"

"I apologize, Brother. I don't know. It could still be near her body, or it may be very far away."

To say this was unhelpful would be a vast understatement. Adams needed answers, and he had the distinct feeling that Stiggens knew more than he was letting on. In truth, Adams just wasn't asking the right questions. Not yet.

"So she could still wake up?" Adams asked.

"There is a chance, yes, but it may be slim."

"But with my help—"

"That isn't something you should say lightly," Stiggens interrupted. "There are many things you don't know yet about the way our universe works. At your current level, there is likely nothing you could accomplish by pursuing this line of thinking. And it could lead you down a very difficult and dangerous path."

"You said you know my situation. Does that mean you understand the largest weight my guilt leaves on me? You understand that it's my fault she's in this situation?"

Stiggens closed his eyes for a moment and took a deep breath. "Yes, Brother. I understand."

"Then you know I can't just sit here while she suffers. I have to do something for her. So I'm begging you to help me."

"The Celestial Code dictates that you speak with the High Council on the matter." Stiggens paused to consider his next words carefully. "I will request an audience on your behalf."

When Adams left Stiggens's quarters, the Realm of the Angels seemed suddenly enormous yet vacuous and lonelier than ever. Adams couldn't stand the idea of returning to his room, but he didn't want to be around others, either. He wandered down hallways—turning corners when he saw someone—and finally came to rest next to an overlook. The flowing stream below seemed soulless, and he wished for a rock to throw into it. No rock appeared in his hand. It was worth a try, he supposed.

His thoughts were out of his control: berating him and making him feel small. He leaned against the railing and put his head down onto his crossed arms. With great effort, he told himself there was hope. There had to be, otherwise what was the point of all this? Despite the thought, he had not even an inkling of how he could help his niece.

What would he say to the High Council? How could he explain how important this was? What he was asking was selfish. He imagined they might tell him it was foolish and unnecessary. Such a request could ruin any respect they may have for him. Perhaps they would take away his additional training with Stiggens. Such was the downward spiral that Sir Pity Party endured.

Just when he thought he couldn't get any lower, that silent voice reached out to comfort him. He had heard it—sensed it—before. Was it his conscience? No, it couldn't be. This voice conveyed thoughts and words through an emotional message in much the same way he had as a Messenger. Its tone was warm and uplifting but also strong and protective. It urged him onward with a promise that his effort would not be in vain.

"I'll try," he responded to the nothingness.

He was just about to force himself to stand up straight when Casey called out to him.

"Are you well?" Casey asked, worry drawing down zir eyebrows. "Did you run into trouble during your assignment?"

For all the effort Adams had gone through to be alone, now that Casey was here, he blurted out everything. Ze was as optimistic as that silent voice had been, assuring Adams that the High Council would listen to his inquiry and consider it seriously.

Ze shared several stories of High Council requests ze had heard of, some rather ridiculous. The High Council seemed to have handled each by a loose interpretation of the Celestial Code, usually favoring to grant the angel's request. For example, one angel had requested the bench outside his door be removed because it made him feel like someone was always surveilling him, though there was no evidence to back his claim. Still, the High Council approved the removal of the bench, and the paranoid angel had to come up with some new conspiracy to complain about.

Adams was thankful to hear of the council's leniency, but Casey's expression still exuded concern.

"Do you really think you can do it, though?" ze asked. "Go into Darkrealm?"

Adams had never heard of Darkrealm before, and he could tell by Casey's disbelief that he maybe, probably, most certainly should have.

"What's Darkrealm?" was the only sensible thing he could say.

He cringed a little at Casey's reaction, which seemed to question if he had done any research before requesting to save his niece.

"You know how the Realm of the Angels is a part of Highrealm, right?" After receiving an affirmative nod from Adams, ze continued. "We are each a collection of energy, and we have a pseudo-physical form here in the Realm of the Angels. In Midrealm, the physical form exists, but a person's soul and spiritual power is actually in another place called Darkrealm. It's a separate level of existence where the spirits of all living things of Midrealm reside. That's a bit simplistic, but does it make sense?"

"I think so, but why do I need to go there?" he asked.

"Well, normally a person's body and soul are tightly tethered between Midrealm and Darkrealm. But when someone goes into a coma, often the tether degrades. Theoretically, you could find her soul in Darkrealm and bring her back to her body. That should allow them to reconnect."

"It's been so long, though," he said. "Almost a year."

"Oh. It may be more serious, then. But we can hope for the best."

"This reconnecting thing. It's been done before, right?"

"Don't worry about it," Casey said, placing a reassuring hand on his shoulder. "We'll figure it out."

He was not reassured.

"I probably shouldn't offer this, but," Casey said, taking a long deep breath before continuing. "Why don't you come to the Archive with me? I can show you the records of the angels who have visited with your family so you can see what's been happening."

"Really?" His heart felt lighter, as if a burden had been lifted.

Ze smiled at Adams's change in mood. "Come on. We can go now."

They walked in silence for a while. Adams's mind drifted off as their steps echoed through the halls. He absently smiled at others as they passed by. His emotional coffers seemed empty, like all the caring he'd been holding onto had now been stripped from him. Like a walking shell, he was temporarily numb to the strong emotions that had overcome him. The halls emptied as they moved beyond the main halls of doors.

A fog began to flow around his feet and ankles, tickling them with a cool grasp. He paused as a chilling gust of mist washed over them. This was someplace he'd never seen before.

"Where are we?" he asked.

"We're near the Southern Training Grounds," Casey replied, gesturing in the direction they were headed. "Fun fact: it's impossible to enter."

Casey sure knew how to pique his curiosity.

"Impossible? Why?"

"A prophecy." Casey smiled, and Adams could sense zir sheer joy at reciting the tale. "The immortals forged these training grounds for the future of Midrealm.

They will serve as a conduit between the angels and immortals. There will come a day when one will be born who may enter the hallowed grounds and will bridge the gap between the physical and non-physical worlds."

This sounded impressive. Of course, Stiggens probably wouldn't think so, but Adams was captivated.

"When will this happen?" Adams couldn't help but ask.

Casey laughed. "You and time." Ze beckoned Adams onward.

"So, when you say impossible, has anyone ever tried?"

"It's said that those who tried were reduced to pure energy. But I've never looked to see if it actually ever happened. If it did, it was probably a long time ago."

The Southern Training Grounds were vast, and the fog only became thicker as they moved around it. Casey explained that several parts of the Realm were fixed, impervious to an individual's perception. These pockets of space were more common further from the living areas. Ze pointed out the dullness of the floors, the plainness of the walls, and the emptiness of the space above them where a sky should be. A large door came into view in the distance, stretching as high as Adams could see and fading into the empty expanse.

"This is the Archive," Casey said as ze pushed open the unfathomably tall doors.

The Archive held all the records of the angels. Every message sent, every report, every trial or inquiry before the High Council, every record of everything was housed here. It appeared as an enormous round room with a large glowing circle in the middle of the floor.

Casey urged Adams to stand within the circle and clear his mind. As soon as he stepped within the boundary, sounds and images began playing all at once, appearing all around him. Casey pulled him back.

"I said clear your mind," ze repeated.

He took a deep breath and remembered the feeling of the fog around his legs. It had been alive somehow, as if it was breathing. The coolness and moistness of the fog had done more than just that, it had given him something. He felt more powerful than he ever had. It provided a brief sense of peace that had escaped him since he died. He smiled a little at the clarity and pushed all the doubts and thoughts from his mind.

He stepped forward.

Images appeared around him and within his mind. He absorbed them and their sounds, but even more so absorbed the emotions attached to them. He allowed them to mix with his own memories, to be engrossed by them, to really live them. And, as tears flowed from his eyes, he felt empowered to do what he must, to bring back his dear niece to her family, and to face the most terrifying thing he'd ever encountered.

It was still difficult for Adams to remove himself from the grasp of time, but it sure seemed like several weeks before he was called upon by the High Council.

They summoned him to the Courts, another region of the Realm that was perceived the same by all angels. From outside, it looked like a small, natural structure. Marble vines tangled together to form walls and stretched upward into nothingness. At the base of the building, the tangles grew outward and downward over a ravine as empty as above. He approached with caution, the entire place seeming to beat as if made from living tissue.

He entered through a large opening and was met by an angel who silently led him to a small chamber. Ze left, and Adams stood quietly until another angel appeared.

Ze smiled gently. "The High Council is ready for you."

Adams nodded and followed zir.

The angel led him through a dark labyrinth of tunnels that widened and narrowed as they twisted their way through it. The ground was soft like grass, and his footsteps made no sounds as he walked. Curious, he put his hand out at a turn and brushed it against the wall. The walls were cold like metal but breathed as if alive, a feeling he couldn't comprehend and had never experienced.

It startled him so much that his guide paused to check on him. He assured zir he was fine, and so they continued the long trek deeper into the belly of the Courts.

They finally emptied into an enormous chamber. Twisted marble vines braided themselves around to form a cavern. They let off a soft glow that lit the large space much more thoroughly than should have been possible. At the center sat the seven members of the High Council—including Brother Stiggens—in a circle.

Adams was so intrigued by his surroundings that he almost didn't notice them.

"Go stand at the center," his guide said, giving him a gentle push forward. "They'll ask you questions. Don't be afraid."

He wasn't afraid, just distracted.

Adams made his way down the slight incline to the center. He was soon surrounded by the most powerful and respected angels of the Realm and realized he didn't know which way to look. He slowly turned and gave a gentle nod to each. They remained silent for a long while, as if speaking amongst themselves in their minds without allowing him access.

Okay, now he was a little scared.

"Welcome, Brother Adams," one finally said. "Please tell us why you are here."

"Oh, I thought . . . I thought you knew," he said.

"We have heard your request from Brother Stiggens. However, a personal request such as this is a delicate matter," an angel behind him said. He turned to look at her. "We would like to hear the request from you."

Adams swallowed down the lump in his throat and stood up straighter, gripped in definite fear.

"My niece has been in a coma for close to a year," he said. "She's the last living relative of my sister. Our family was small, and our parents are dead. I'd like to be given the chance to descend into Darkrealm and repair the tether to my niece's soul so that she may live again."

"Descend into Darkrealm?" an angel behind him said, and he spun to face him. "Do you even understand what that means? You haven't completed your training yet."

"It's true I have a lot to learn," Adams said. "But I'm not afraid."

"You don't even know what there is to fear." He turned again to face this voice. "Darkrealm isn't just another realm. You can't use your power the same way there. You can't protect yourself. And Darkrealm is full of Whispers, shadows that seek to seduce you into despair, to make you become one of them. Your very existence would be endangered."

He was shaking. What they were describing sounded like a nightmare. Maybe Stiggens was right. Perhaps there really was nothing he could do. But Adams was nothing if not persistent. The thought of Illeina being trapped there with these Whispers sobered him.

"I'm willing to risk my existence for her. I love her as if she's my own child." His voice came out as determined as he had hoped, without an inkling of his body's trembling.

"Adams," Stiggens spoke up, a slight sense of warning in his tone. Adams turned to him. "Tell them the truth of your motives."

Adams looked at each face again, and he knew they were already aware. He put his hands together to ease their quivering. Tears came to his eyes, but he forced them back. He swallowed back a sob, cursing the guilt that stayed with him always.

"It's my fault she's in a coma," he said reluctantly.

"What you mean to say is, you blame yourself," Stiggens corrected.

What followed were the voices of dismissal.

"So, we are to grant you this request because of your guilt?"

"We all feel the weight of the guilt."

"We can't grant every request to ease a conscience."

Their voices pounded down upon him. He clasped his fists hard as they slammed their doubts into his soul, each like a knife through the heart. Then, when they'd said far more than enough, they went silent. He stood, head down, fists so tight that his nails were digging into his palms.

"I understand," he mumbled, his voice cracking.

"Brother Adams," a voice of one of the High Council came from behind him. He couldn't bring himself to turn to face her. "Upon Brother Stiggens' request, we investigated the record of fate for Illeina, your niece. We are bound by the Celestial Code not to interfere with those with determined fates, especially when this means to deny death to those who are fated to die.

"Despite her dire situation, Illeina's fate seems to be in flux."

He raised his head and asked, "Flux? What does that mean?"

"It's a rarity, Brother," another voice spoke. "She is not fated to die, yet she is not fated to accomplish anything in life. She is a mystery to Fate."

A mystery to Fate? Adams wasn't sure whether to be happy or terrified.

"Because of this," another voice said, "we will allow you to attempt to re-tether her soul."

Energy restored, Adams turned to the voice who spoke and bowed to zir. "Thank you."

"However," ze added. He looked up at zir. "You are not powerful or experienced enough to handle the obstacles of Darkrealm, and so we will not allow you to go alone."

This was alarming. If Darkrealm was as dangerous as they said, anyone who joined him could be lost.

"I'm not prepared to risk anyone else's existence," Adams said.

"Friend Casey has volunteered," Stiggens said. "Ze will accompany you to Darkrealm and assist you in restoring Illeina to life."

A lump built up in his throat, and as much as he wanted to protest, he never got the chance.

"We will expect a report of your attempt once you complete the task," Stiggens said. "Be aware that there is no guarantee you'll succeed."

Another voice, the last, said, "You are dismissed."

Sitting silently in a quiet clearing of the Northern Training Grounds, Adams tried to keep his breathing slow and steady, still shaking off the nervous energy that his meeting with the High Council had evoked. His perceived heartbeat was racing, and it seemed as real to him as the anxiety that accompanied it. With very little idea of what to expect from Darkrealm—aside from the High

Council's terrifying tidbits—he was unsure if he could do anything to help if something happened to Casey.

Why ze would volunteer for something like this still baffled him.

When he had left the High Council, Casey had been waiting for him. He immediately asked zir what ze was thinking.

"I have the experience to help you," Casey said. "And I want to help Illeina, too."

"Have you been to Darkrealm before?" Adams asked, but Casey smiled without answering.

"There are many more important questions," ze said with a laugh. "Like where and how are we going to enter Darkrealm?"

Casey had explained to Adams that it was difficult to transfer their energy into Darkrealm. To move between Highrealm and Midrealm, a transfer of energy was simple. There were countless transfer points in Midrealm that accepted energy from Highrealm and allowed it to pass through. Some areas were more sparse than others, but a transfer point was always nearby, especially with the speeds that angels could travel in Midrealm.

Darkrealm was different in many ways. The tethers between Midrealm and Darkrealm were everywhere, or more accurately, were truly ubiquitous, almost as if Darkrealm coated Midrealm like jelly on bread, sitting just offset but universally connected. Even so, transfer points were rare.

They would need to find one of these connections to cross over into Darkrealm. Casey seemed to think that the Archive held information about the location of portals between Midrealm and Darkrealm, but also cautioned that portals wandered over time. They would have to look for slight disturbances in the energy flow in Midrealm.

Once in Darkrealm, their powers would be almost useless. They couldn't move their energy quickly through space as they could in Midrealm. They couldn't gather matter or energy to protect themselves, and they couldn't effectively communicate with emotions. It would almost be as if they were mortal again. Although they couldn't lose their existence, things called Whispers could manipulate them and change the essence of their being, turning them into Whispers themselves.

"Why are they called Whispers?" Adams had asked.

"They represent all the things you think but would never say. They use that to influence you. For an ambitious person, that could mean stepping on those below you to get to the top. For a violent person, succumbing to a Whisper can mean abusing or killing someone. If you become one, you'll lose your individuality and will be lost forever."

When he asked, Casey had admitted ze wasn't certain how to evade or stop the Whispers from influencing someone.

"We'll just have to be careful and stay together. Hopefully, we can help each other," Casey said with a smile.

Yeah, right.

Despite the wonder of the training grounds around him, Adams's anxiety grew as he wondered how the

Whispers could affect him. He was still struggling with his guilt, which left him highly susceptible to being influenced. There was no more time for training, no more time to learn how to protect himself. He had to trust in Casey and zir ability.

He turned his attention to Illeina. Where could her soul be in Darkrealm? If Darkrealm mirrored Midrealm, perhaps she would go somewhere familiar: a playground she liked, his old apartment, her home, the fairgrounds where he had often taken her for events. Casey had been confident that ze could find a portal in a central location and had sent him off to calm himself, which wasn't quite working out as well as he'd hoped.

When he stopped trying to think about, well, all that, his mind was overwhelmed with the sights and sounds of his accident. Illeina had ridden with him on his motorcycle many times before. The first time was when she was five. She was all giggles as he held her against him and rode in small, slow circles around the cul-de-sac just outside her home.

By the time she was seven, they were riding short distances such as to the store or to school. When she was nine, they took their first road trip on the bike, to a camping ground they had visited several times before. He always took extra precautions. He was always overly cautious about those around him.

That morning was only different in one way. One small mistake had resulted in deadly repercussions. He so vividly remembered the feel of the handles in his palms and of Illeina's hands clutching him tightly.

He could smell the moisture that hung in the air, ready to rain at any moment. He saw the street lights blinking. He was seeing the headlights of a car.

His weight being thrown.

Bones cracking.

Blood, so much blood. Was he already dead by then?

Feet rushing around him.

People crying as they saw Illeina and screaming for someone to call for help.

It was as if it was happening at this very moment.

CHAPTER 4

Adams snapped his eyes open and shook off the tears rushing to them. It was the first time he had relived the crash this vividly since he found out Illeina was alive. He could still barely believe it was true, even after seeing all the angels' reports, even after hearing it from his sister's mouth.

Perhaps Illeina was spared for a reason. Perhaps she wasn't meant to die. She was a kind child, always the first to want to help someone. She could see a person's pain when others were completely oblivious to it.

Yet she was also strong-willed. If she thought you were wrong, she told you. If she wanted to do something, it was next to impossible to talk her out of it. Whenever she threw a fit for not getting her way, he always had the same joke: "Thank goodness you're such a good girl, because you'd make one hell of a super villain."

She was also the biggest fan of the consortium he was a part of to draft global peace policies. He and

Amanda often joked that Illeina would someday take it over and show the world who was boss. He always assumed she was going to do great things for the world.

If that was true, then it was up to him, with Casey's help, to make sure she fulfilled her destiny.

All of the angelic realm brimmed with tension, as if Adams's angst was in harmony with the universe itself. The silent voice that sometimes spoke to him was whispering where no one could hear. In the forbidden Southern Training Grounds, the fog swirled around itself. Twisting and churning, folding in on itself, it expanded and condensed, speaking a language of its own.

Its activity caught the eye of Casey when ze left the Archive.

Zir search for a portal to Darkrealm was fruitless, but after a break, ze would continue undeterred. Ze knew these portals were uncommon, just as ze knew they couldn't be easily detected. They couldn't be seen or felt, however once you went through, you could tell. The world of Darkrealm looked much like Midrealm, but with an otherworldly aura. From Darkrealm, the portals were visible, like doorways of reflected light distorting what lay beyond.

It had taken zir a long time to sort through what ze remembered from the literature. There were many explanations from angels about their chance encounters with Darkrealm. Most often, they had stumbled into a portal accidentally, immediately realizing their powers were muffled. As taught during training, they paused to look around. Usually not far from the portal, they identified the entrance and left, noted the location, and then went on their way.

There were very rare occasions when an angel went into Darkrealm intentionally. One particularly explorative angel had set out to map all the entrances to Darkrealm. The High Council hadn't approved of her endeavor, yet she persisted. She hadn't gotten very far when she was found out and punished. When she returned from her punishment, she tried again. It was on her third trip into Darkrealm that she was influenced by the Whispers and became one of them.

As they say, when you play with fire, you get burnt. Or turned into a scary supernatural creature.

Casey didn't deny to zirself that ze was afraid. Going to Darkrealm didn't seem worth it. Illeina had been in a coma for long enough that Casey was certain she had wandered far from her body, untethered. If that was the case, re-tethering her might prove impossible. Casey also understood that after so long untethered, even if they were able to repair the damage, Illeina wouldn't be the same. Her psyche was likely so tattered that she wouldn't be able to function in society anymore.

Even so, it pained Casey to see Adams in such dismay. Ze couldn't imagine loving someone as much as Adams loved his niece, to be willing to risk so much for her. Yet here ze was, putting zirself at risk for him.

Ze enjoyed Adams's company, looked forward to seeing him, and was often amused by him. Ze valued their relationship. Ze wasn't deaf to the whispers of angels around zir. Casey knew that ze was strange to them.

Yet Adams never questioned it, never even took notice of it.

No. It wasn't that he didn't notice, but that he chose to ignore it. It made Casey smile to think about it.

Now, as both of their existences teetered at the edge of extinction, ze wondered what Adams's feelings were. Did Adams treasure zir as ze treasured him? And why was he truly going to Darkrealm? Did he really think he could save Illeina? Or was he hoping to be influenced by the Whispers?

A strained voice called out to zir, and ze turned to look. Ze was just passing the fog filled entrance of the Southern Training Grounds. The wind howled, sounding strangely like a voice, as if a warning.

"I feel it, too," Casey said to the lifeless fog. "Please, watch over us."

Later on—after finally finding a clue that could lead them to a portal, inexplicably adjacent to a recipe for clam chowder—Casey found Adams in the Northern Training Grounds. Ze sat next to him, and they shared a silent moment.

Casey took his hand gently. It felt warm, alive—though ze was under no delusion that either of them was living. Casey couldn't help but wonder if it was Adams's projection or zir own perception of him that gave off this warmth, but it was comforting. Casey longed to stay in this moment and not witness Adams disappear to the Whispers, as ze so feared.

One thing was clear, though. Adams needed to do this, and the Realm of the Angels vibrated with the excitement and fear of it. This was destiny, and there was nothing either of them could do to stop it now.

"I found a portal, maybe," ze said. "It's near Illeina's hospital, and from what I can tell, it seems to drift less than others."

Adams's face gave away his feelings of guilt. "You shouldn't be going with me, Casey."

"You won't make it back if I don't."

"But what if **you** don't. What if—"

Casey interrupted by putting zir hand to Adams's lips. Ze shook zir head. "Let's just not have this conversation." Ze smiled. "If it makes you feel better, there are things about me that you don't know . . . that make me less susceptible to Whispers and their influence. I'm the best person to accompany you, and I'll be an asset to you in Darkrealm."

"You're lying to make me feel better," Adams argued.

Casey shook zir head. "I'd never lie about something like this. I'm telling you the truth. I swear."

Adams's disbelieving expression bordered on comedy. "And it's something you can't teach me?"

Casey shook zir head again.

That seemed to be enough to placate him. "Then I guess it does make me feel a little better. But don't put yourself at more risk because of it, alright?"

"I promise," Casey replied, and ze truly meant it. "Shall we go? The High Council said we are free to leave at our convenience."

They appeared at one of the back entrances of the hospital. Adams looked around, somewhat hoping the Darkrealm portal would be immediately visible. It wasn't.

After a moment to get zir bearings, Casey pointed. "It's on the east side. Let's go."

"Through?" Adams asked.

Sure, he had gone through a few walls now, but he still preferred to go through doorways when possible. It just seemed unnatural, like petting a cat backwards.

Casey gave him a concerned look, then put a hand to zir mouth as ze tried not to laugh. "Are you still in your 'I only use doors' phase?"

"You don't find it strange?" Adams asked.

"It's just a wall. You can see through them when you want to, right?"

Adams nodded shyly.

"So, why not walk through them?"

Adams didn't answer because, well, he didn't have any reasoning aside from the idea giving him the heebie-jeebies.

Luckily, Casey was empathetic, although possibly a bit patronizing. "Okay, look. It's unlikely the portal is inside the building, since energy fluctuations are more prevalent in high traffic areas. Why don't we go around the building, in case we run into it?"

Adams didn't mind being patronized in this instance, especially if it meant not going through a wall.

Once they reached the other side of the building, they split up.

"Remember," Casey said, "if you happen to pass into Darkrealm, you'll notice things look different. Immediately turn around, and you'll see the portal. Just come back through to get me."

"I will," Adams promised.

The hours dragged by, Adams anxiety rising with each passing step. He couldn't believe there was no better way to search. What were all these heavenly powers for if he couldn't use it to find portals to otherworldly and possibly terrifying realms?

He kept his mind open to energy shifts, but he sensed nothing. He could tell that Casey was a few hundred meters away and that there were trees and cars and people between them. He let his mind wander a moment, focusing instead on where to search for Illeina once they were in Darkrealm. It seemed logical to start at her family home. Perhaps she'd go back there and look for her parents.

Then he remembered something. The week before the accident, Illeina had heard about a new entertainment center that was opening. She had called him as soon as she got home from school. He was still at work and typically didn't receive personal calls unless it was an emergency. He rushed to answer, assuming his sister needed his help.

"Amanda, what's wrong?" he had answered.

"It's me, Uncle. It's me," Illeina sang with a laugh.

He sighed. "Is everything okay? You shouldn't call me while I'm at work."

"But Uncle," she whined.

"Baby, it's okay. What's wrong?"

She had taken a deep breath in before replying, "Sam said that a place is going to open next week, and I didn't even know about it, but I really want to go, and I was afraid I'd forget if I didn't call you right away and I know how sometimes you get busy so I wanted to make sure to reserve the time now because some other kids are going this Saturday but I'd rather wait until next Saturday and go with you and—"

"Illeina, take a breath." He smiled, refreshed by her enthusiasm. "What kind of place is it? Like a mall or something?"

"Like an arcade, but cooler!"

"And you don't want to go with your friends this weekend?"

"No, I want to go with you. You're the most fun!"

Even though she had just had her birthday party, he couldn't help himself.

"Okay, I'll tell you what. If you promise not to call me at work again unless it's an emergency, I'll take you."

"Really, you will?!" she screeched, as if he didn't always give her what she wanted.

"Of course, princess."

"Thank you thank you thank you!" she screamed. "Uncle, you're the best ever. We're going to have the best time. I just know it!"

60

He hadn't been able to get her off the phone until she had laid out all the fun things she wanted to do. That was a less than productive afternoon, to put it mildly, but her joy was infectious.

Adams couldn't believe he had forgotten about the entertainment center. Shouldn't angels have perfect memories or something? Without reason, he found himself sure she would be there. His mind began racing ahead to what they might find, yet he forced himself to return to the present. After realizing his hands were trembling, he looked around for a place he could calm down. A nearby bench caught his eye, so he sat and leaned forward to place his elbows on his knees.

During the week after she had decided to go to this place, Illeina had given excruciating details about everything they were going to do. She had very high expectations for him, and he'd been exhausted just from listening to her. And though he was impressed at her planning, he harbored lingering concerns that she was not fitting in well with the other kids.

"She's fine," Amanda had promised him when he brought it up to her. "Every day, she comes home with stories about her friends, and they call and talk to her often. She just really loves you."

"If you're sure."

Amanda had placed her hand in his and stroked it gently. It had always comforted him when they held hands, ever since they were kids.

"I'm sure. Now, why don't you stop worrying about her social life and start worrying about your own."

61

He snatched his hand away so he could cross his arms. "Don't start again," he said with a groan.

"Illeina needs some cousins on our side of the family, don't you think? And you know what needs to happen."

"Any time I spend dating is less time I can spend with her."

"Like you don't go on dates," Amanda teased. "I'm not stupid. I know you've played the field. You just never settle down."

Before he could argue, Illeina ran into the room.

"What're you talking about?" she begged. "Tell me. Tell me."

"Your mom wants me to find a partner so I can't spend time with you," he said.

Illeina turned to her mother, cheeks puffed out. "No, Mommy! No! I'm going to stay with Uncle forever, because we're the most fun together!"

Amanda had just laughed before scooping her daughter up for giggles and kisses.

Adams sighed at the memory, a strong sigh—the kind that really makes you feel empty inside. Adams didn't have time for weak sighs. After all, if anyone was watching—for example, the source of a certain silent voice that spoke to him on occasion—he needed them to know just how despondent he was.

Illeina would never have cousins, or even her beloved Uncle. But at least she would have her life. He leaned against the back of the bench, dropping his head to look up at the sky.

But the sky was suddenly streaked with reds and purples, and his power was reduced to nothing. He jumped to his feet.

His power returned. Had he imagined it? It was as if the world was completely silent, and he had struggled against gravity to be free from its grasp.

He took a few steps away from the bench and looked around. Everything was back to normal, at least as far as he could tell.

Casey appeared beside him. "What happened? I couldn't feel your presence a moment ago. Did you find it?"

He snapped his head to look at zir. "What? No. I mean, I don't know. Something weird just happened when I sat on the bench."

Casey looked him over, then stared at the bench. Ze put a knee on the seat and leaned forward. Zir top half disappeared, causing Adams to jump backward. Ze leaned back, reappearing.

"It's Darkrealm," ze said, as if it was the most obvious thing ever.

It hadn't been obvious to Adams.

Ze crossed zir arms to hold zirself. "It's cold and strange, isn't it?"

Adams nodded, and reached out to put a hand on zir shoulder.

Zir gaze drifted to the ground. "It never changes."

Adams knew better than to ask what that meant. "Are you okay?" he asked instead.

Ze nodded, letting go of zirself, as if it would remove what ze was feeling. "Darkrealm sits offset from the world a bit, almost as if it's sitting just above. So, you sometimes have to step or climb up to cross into it. Some portals lay closer to the ground, but not this one. Ground level is above the top of the bench."

That explained why Adams had felt like his head was detached from his body, ready to roll away to explore a new world. He silently thanked it for not moving on without the rest of him.

"Have you decided where we're going?" Casey asked.

"Yes, it's a couple miles west of here. A place she wanted to go."

Ze nodded again, but didn't make a move to enter the portal. So, Adams took the initiative. He stepped up onto the bench and leaned forward, bracing himself against its back. Around him, just at his shoulder, was a strange glow. He looked down, where he could see a wobbly version of his hands, still in Midrealm. The glow emanated around him, as if pulling its surroundings down and into the portal he was standing in. In front of him was a ledge, which he used to pull himself up through the portal. Layers seemed to peel away from him as he pushed off of the bench, tossing himself up onto the ledge behind it. It was as if the portal was stripping off everything of his being except his soul.

So, this was Darkrealm.

At first glance, it looked like where they had been before. But something about the colors of the world made his head hurt, as if colors didn't exist here—or perhaps his angelic brain was struggling to comprehend them. The nearby trees, the rocks, even the bench seemed to pulse with life. Creatures nearby, insects and lizards, glowed as they rushed away. And the people who passed by him were phantoms of themselves, some more translucent than others and all with a glow trailing behind them.

Most disturbing of all, there was a strong sense that eyes were watching him, coming from every direction.

Casey thanked him when he helped zir through the portal and then gestured west. "This way, right?" ze asked.

"Yeah," he replied, eyes wandering to try to identify their observers.

"Stay focused, Adams," Casey insisted. "Spacing out will only lead to trouble. I know it feels odd, but you have to focus on your task."

"Of course," he replied. "Let's go."

He said that, but every step felt like a massive effort. He had been in the Realm of the Angels for a long time and had adapted to the feeling of freedom there. Instead of being forced to walk due to gravitational pull and a long history of evolution, he chose to walk in the angelic realm. And this place felt similar in a way, unencumbered by forces like gravity, yet he felt weighed down in a different way. He imagined this was how it would feel to be held to the ground by string or rope while his body longed to fly skyward.

Did this make him a balloon? Or perhaps a puppet? He wasn't quite sure, and neither sounded like fun.

On the plus side, his senses were heightened. He saw creatures everywhere, felt every blade of grass and grain of sand under his bare feet. He heard every movement of the wind, smelled every molecule of mist. He sensed those eyes on him, from everywhere. They pierced his body and crept deep into his mind. He forcefully tried to push them out, to guard himself and concentrate.

Instead, his mind betrayed him—because minds are good at that. The crash replayed itself over and over. It reminded him that it was his fault Illeina was untethered and drifting away from her body.

His mind shifted suddenly to memories of the Realm of the Angels, of meeting Casey, going out to "late night" parties, dancing and cheering and singing. He had allowed himself so much freedom, so much healing. Even his selfless friend, Casey, had done so much for him while he let Illeina rot in a hospital bed.

He was despicable. Irredeemable. He didn't deserve to exist, much less be an angel. Why had he become an angel in the first place? Probably because he felt high and mighty, full of hubris.

No, that couldn't be right. He had become an angel because no other choice suited him, right? Joining with the source would just tarnish that energy. Reincarnating would just push the world into darkness with his filth.

He no longer remembered which was the truth. Either way, he was a waste of space and energy.

Illeina's tiny form appeared before him, on the ground and dripping wet in dark, stained red. She cried out for him. Blood rained down on her. She cried blood. She drooled blood.

He dropped to his knees and tried to gather her in his arms, but she screamed at him to get away.

"Leave me alone! Stop hurting me!"

Jumping away from her, he hurried to his feet and ran.

He was always running away. Always pushing away the responsibility. How he wished to be removed from this hell, to forget everything!

Something grabbed his legs, and he fell forward onto his face. He thrashed and turned over to fight his attacker. Blackness encompassed him. He cried out. The blackness grabbed his face, and terror gripped him.

He trembled. He cried out.

It was all over. He had failed.

CHAPTER 5

Though Adams felt lost in darkness, a sudden slap across his face brought him to his senses. He grabbed at his cheek. When he next opened his eyes, he was lying on the ground with Casey standing over him.

His eyes grew wide as sweat—real sweat—rolled down the curves of his body. Casey held zir hand up, ready to hit him again, but ze paused as he made no attempt to move or flee.

"Adams?" ze asked.

"What happened?" he breathed.

"The Whispers. They had you within their grasp. They crept into your mind. I almost lost you." Casey knelt and pulled Adams close. "You scared me."

He tried to stammer a reply but found it difficult to find the words. He hadn't seen any Whispers, nor did he know how they could have snuck up on him.

"I didn't notice until it was too late," ze continued, "but the Whispers surrounded us. They already had their talons in you, but you seemed fine. Just a little quiet. And then you were gone. I screamed and screamed, but you didn't hear me."

"So you hit me?" Adams asked, finally piecing things together.

"Of course I hit you," Casey said, giving him a small smack. "What else was I supposed to do? You would have turned into a Whisper if I hadn't!"

"Hitting me actually worked?"

Casey smiled and cried, hugging Adams and calling him an idiot. Then, with a sudden sobriety, ze turned off the waterworks and said, "We should leave."

Adams let Casey help him up. "Why am I sweaty?"

"You aren't. That's a byproduct of the change. Whispers have an emulsive texture. You were becoming one, so you were changing."

"It's . . . sticky," he said with a sigh, trying desperately to shake it off.

"It'll fade. Don't worry," Casey replied, grabbing his arm and pulling him along.

It didn't take much effort to get him moving. Still a bit rattled, he was happy to get as far from these Whispers as possible.

It didn't feel as long as it took to get to the entertainment center, probably because Adams was preoccupied by his gummy and squelching steps. Zero stars. Would not recommend.

The whole building pulsed with activity. Figures of all ages filtered in and out, spirits tethered to people in Midrealm. Adams and Casey approached from the back, and used an open door to enter. The place was packed, and Adams struggled to find a way around the crowd. He tried to focus on the glowing wisps that trailed behind them. The wisps flowed together and swirled around, as if creating an energetic excitement that spread out from each person.

Before he realized it, he was running, with Casey at his heels. They searched around games, in the children's play area, and at the bowling alley, but saw no sign of Illeina. Adams slowed as they reached the end of their search, eyes frantically going back and forth.

"I don't see her," he said.

"Maybe she's not here."

"No, she's here . . . somewhere."

"You're certain?"

"Yes. I just know," Adams demanded. "I know she's here."

They looked around, again and again, going in circles for what could have been hours. Who can really tell in Darkrealm? If time worked differently in Highrealm, it was probably just as warped—if not more so—in this nightmare realm.

Despite all their effort, Illeina was not inside. And finally, Casey insisted they try somewhere else.

"We've looked everywhere," Casey said. "At this point, we're doing her a disservice by staying here."

"Maybe you're right," Adams replied with a disgruntled moan.

"At least, let's go outside for a little while. I'd like to get my bearings."

He'd completely disregarded Casey's feelings. This must have been difficult for zir as well. Guilt crept into his thoughts. "Yes, of course."

He felt despondent and empty again. He pushed the feelings away, and as he did so, something shifted within him. Whatever it was—and there were no words that could explain it—the difference was apparent when he saw them. Whispers. They were dark, darker than black somehow, with glowing red eyes. They moved quickly, but in a way Adams could only describe as oozing.

The Whispers hovered around and between the crowds. They seemed content with others and paid him no attention. But he could feel them, too, in a way he hadn't when they attacked him. Had they changed him somehow? He tried to pin down what part of him had been altered. It was on the tip of his tongue, like the name of the lead actor in that movie you saw the other day.

It had something to do with his angelic power, he realized. That gave him pause. He was definitely sensing a power that he couldn't feel earlier, a power he shouldn't have while in Darkrealm. But whatever this power was, it was beyond his reach.

When they left through the doors of the entertainment center, Casey grabbed his arm and stopped him.

Following zir gaze, he looked across the pavement, along the exterior wall of the building, to a bench that was strangely devoid of those living wisps he had become familiar with.

Instead of a crowd of living souls, a small child he recognized all too well sat, looking left and right, talking to herself. She laughed, bringing warmth and joy to his heart. Then, abruptly, she was crying.

He took a step toward her, only to be held back by Casey's hand grasping his arm.

"Wait," Casey hissed in a low whisper.

"It's Illeina, Casey," he insisted. "She's right here, waiting for me, just like I said."

Casey's expression was tight and serious, and he couldn't help but question his most basic assumption.

"Is it not her?" he asked.

"It's her," Casey replied. "But she's been here a long time. She may not be herself."

"What do you mean? You didn't mention anything like this before."

"That's because I wasn't sure. But you can tell by looking at her. Something's off."

"Even so, she's still my niece. She'll still know me."

"That's what I'm trying to say, Adams," ze insisted, grip tightening. "I don't think she'll recognize you at all. And she has power here that we don't. So, be cautious." Ze said those last two words in as patronizing a tone as ze ever, but zir eyes were locked on his. Zir iron hold on his arm was painful.

73

He nodded, and Casey removed zir hand from his arm—though not zir "I'm watching you" stare.

After just a few steps in her direction, Illeina's head snapped to look at Adams. She was wearing her hospital gown, and she shook her arm back and forth so that her hospital bracelet made a rhythmic, plastic-y sound. Adams paused mid-step.

She stared long and hard, eyes wide and shaking her arm rhythmically before becoming bored with the staring contest and returning to her odd business. Adams looked back at Casey, but ze just stood back, holding zir-self, watching with increasing apprehension. He took a few more steps toward his niece.

Her bright blue eyes were back on him, wide and worried, shaking her arm faster while her hospital bracelet rang out to its swishing beat.

"Illeina?" he said softly.

She screamed, a loud screeching that made the space around her bend and warp, pulsing with the power of it. It was too loud to speak, so Adams reached out to Casey with his mind.

"How can she do this?" he thought to Casey.

"I don't know," Casey replied in thought. "She shouldn't be able to."

The air shook, knocking them both backward. Casey let out a surprised yelp as ze hit the ground. Another shock wave sent Adams down as well. Illeina paused, seeming content with the state of things. Unsure what else to do, he tried speaking to the young girl again.

"Illeina," Adams called. "It's me."

"I don't know you," Illeina yelled. "Leave me alone!"

"It's me, your Uncle!"

"No, no! I'm waiting! Don't take me away! I'll scream!"

He paused to think. The new, powerful feeling he had sensed earlier remained just beyond his reach, and he felt an urge to use it. He reached at it with his mind, asking for its help. As if standing on his mind's tippy toes, he reached, rolling slowly up onto the figurative edge of his reach.

Suddenly, a bright power shot from his chest toward Illeina. He cried out as it enveloped her. It swirled and spun, then a vertical light reached down from the sky, shot through her and into the ground.

"How are you doing this?" Casey asked.

"What did I do?" he replied.

Ze was still sitting on the ground, and it didn't look like ze was in a hurry to get up. Given zir reluctance, he stayed down as well because you can't be knocked down if you're on the ground. At least, he hoped not.

"It's a spell," ze responded. "The one I was going to use to see if we could help Illeina."

"What do you mean **if** we could help her? I thought we just had to take her back to her body."

A loud boom thundered around them, and a shock wave rolled outward beneath them. Adams covered his head with his arms, shielding himself. The bright light condensed down into a bright point. It then faded, just as Illeina's screeching cry returned.

"We have a problem," Casey said, but couldn't hear zirself over the child's wail. Casey continued in thought, "We have to go back."

"I'm not leaving without her," Adams replied.

"We **have to**! I'll explain everything, but we don't have a choice right now."

Adams cringed as Illeina's scream grew louder. He put his hands to his ears, but it didn't dull the sound. Allowing Casey to help him to his feet, he felt helpless, and the emotion only deepened as they hurried away.

Illeina stopped screaming. Smiling at her success, she returned to her private conversation.

Adams probed for an explanation as Casey led him back to Midrealm, but ze refused to speak. It wasn't until they were through the portal that Casey allowed zirself to pause. Ze breathed a sigh of relief at being back in a familiar realm, placing zir hands on zir knees and letting zir head hang limply.

It looked like ze was holding a tiny pity party, maybe the tiniest because after only a minute, ze looked up at Adams and shook zir head.

"I'm sorry. I was hoping it wouldn't come to this," Casey said.

"What are you talking about?" Adams asked. "We just need to calm her down and take her back to her body. It should be that simple. You said it was that simple." As the weight of his guilt seemed to return in full force, he grappled with his mind to stay focused. "We should be able to save her." He fought to stop his hands from shaking and for his tears to stay in his eyes where they belonged.

Casey grabbed his shoulders.

"Don't do this, Adams. You have to keep control." At a gentle nod from him, ze continued. "Now, tell me what happened back there. How were you able to do that spell?"

"I don't know," Adams admitted freely and then repeated. "I don't know. I just wanted so badly to help her, and then it happened." He paused, wondering if he should share about the power he'd felt. "Casey." How could he say in words what he was feeling? His mind spun in circles as he tried to form sentences. "What if, when the Whispers attacked me, what if they did something to me?"

"Did something? Like what?"

"Well, what if, somehow, almost being turned into a Whisper changed me? Something within me is different, more powerful. But I didn't know how to tap into it until I saw Illeina."

"I've never heard of someone almost becoming a Whisper and coming back. I didn't even know it was possible until we did it," Casey confessed.

"I didn't say anything at the time," Adams continued, "but at the arcade, I could see the Whispers. I could see them following people, watching them, speaking to them. Could you see them?"

Casey shook zir head. "I only saw shadows of them while they were trying to take you. And they

77

seemed delayed somehow, as if I was seeing the memory of them. That's why I went after you instead of them, because they're almost invisible." Ze considered this, then asked, "This new power. Do you still feel it?" Adams nodded, and Casey tried to formulate a hypothesis. Failing miserably, ze sighed. "This is crazy."

"I think there's something crazier," Adams said. "I think Illeina's being controlled by a Whisper, too."

"What?" ze exclaimed "Why?"

"When she screamed and did . . . whatever she was doing, I could feel it. The same sensation as when the Whispers tried to change me. And I don't know, Casey, I could just **tell**. That's why she could do those things. And maybe it's also why she doesn't remember me."

Casey put a hand to Adams's face and forced him to look at zir. "No, Adams. This is wishful thinking. She was untethered. She probably should have faded away by now."

"What do you mean?" Adams argued. "I thought if she was separated from her body, we could just bring her back and re-tether her."

Casey took a deep breath and stroked Adams's cheek gently. Then, frustrated, ze removed the hand and ran zir fingers through zir hair.

"Do you remember the strange fog you saw around people? The glow. You saw that, right? Those were the shadows of the tethers that connect all life to its physical body in Midrealm. When someone is in a coma, those tethers fade. If there was even the slightest link, we could bring her back to her body and there would be a good chance she'd come out of her coma. That isn't the case with Illeina. That spell you did, its purpose is to detect that link and amplify it so it's visible, but it faded to nothingness. There's nothing left of her tether."

"So, what do we do now?" he asked.

"I don't know, Adams." Ze shook zir head, mouth open as if ze had something more to say. But nothing came.

"We have to try something. She's still there. She was right there." A lump built at the back of his throat.

This couldn't be the end. If Illeina still existed in Darkrealm, there had to be a way to save her. Casey remained silent for a long time, and Adams patiently waited for any answer at all.

"I've heard," Casey said reluctantly, "that there is a way to re-tether someone. I don't know how to do it, but we could ask one of the older angels."

It was all the hope Adams needed.

"Great," he cheered, "let's go to Brother Stiggens, and—"

"Wait," ze interrupted him. "Listen to me."

Ze waited until he was looking right into zir eyes before continuing.

"Re-tethering someone who has been untethered is not without consequences. She won't be the same. Surely you've heard of people coming out of comas after a long time and having severe mental health issues. Is that really something you want to risk?"

Adams didn't answer. He couldn't find any words to express how much he needed this hope. Still, Casey continued.

"You're dead now, Adams. It isn't so bad, right? You've seen what awaits her. She can join with the Source and be one with all of us."

Still he remained silent.

Ze waited a long while, but finally sighed and said, "Let's go see Brother Stiggens. We can figure everything else out after speaking with him."

Stiggens acted surprised when Adams and Casey arrived at his door, despite Casey probably informing him telepathically as soon as they arrived in the Realm of the Angels. He welcomed them into his quarters, which appeared as an outdoor courtyard with a fountain at the center. Several large pillows were scattered around the floor in a haphazard seating arrangement, and the scent of lavender drifted through the air. At Stiggens' insistence, they all sat on the floor and exchanged pleasantries.

They explained at length the situation they had encountered in Darkrealm. Stiggens seemed unphased at hearing that the Whispers had taken hold of an untethered soul. In fact, Stiggens claimed this was normal for wandering spirits that ended up in Darkrealm.

"It was one of the concerns we had about you going to that wretched place," he explained. "Untethered spirits are often easily influenced because they still have things they want, yet they often don't remember details about their life."

"How do we get her away from the Whisper?" Adams asked.

"You have to force the Whisper to give up its hold on her," Casey answered, understanding somehow what needed to be done.

Stiggens showed his agreement with a nod. Adams couldn't believe what he was hearing. Was he going to have to fight this thing in hand-to-hand combat or something? There was no way he could win something like that.

"What does that entail?"

Casey replied, "There was one angel who claimed to have disrupted the hold a Whisper had by using the vessel's power against it. They reached into the vessel's mind and triggered a memory of some kind. But they did so from Midrealm, where they had use of their power."

"I can use my power in Darkrealm," Adams said.

Stiggens was undeterred. "You can't rely on that, I'm afraid. You don't have the training to even attempt—"

"No one has the training," Adams interrupted. "No one else has done this. Am I wrong?"

Stiggens and Casey shared a look. Adams didn't appreciate the look one bit.

"I can see the Whispers," he continued. "I can find the one controlling her and figure out some way to get it to release its grip. Teach me how to do that, and I'll figure out how to do it in Darkrealm."

Stiggens searched Adams's face for any hint of hesitation, but there was none.

"If you must," was all Stiggens could say. He sighed, and with a groan, rolled his body into a more comfortable position. "You've already learned every-thing we could teach you that would help you defeat it."

"But I don't know how to fight it," Adams said.

"Neither do I," Stiggens replied. "The skills we covered in our basic training are the basis for all that we do. You'll have to figure it out from there. But, Brother, I must ask, what will you do after? She's untethered."

"I've heard," Casey suddenly spoke up, "there's a spell that can be used to re-tether a soul and its body."

Stiggens looked long and hard at Casey with an un-comfortable silence. Adams didn't like this look either, but he didn't know what it meant and was too polite to ask.

"This is not something I consider lightly," Stiggens grumbled slowly. "Why not let it be? There will be many negative ramifications. Your niece won't be the same."

"I know, I know," Adams argued. "Everyone keeps telling me that as if I don't know, but I do. I understand that her mind will be different and that she may struggle in life. But she'll be alive."

That silent whisper that often came to him was with him now, encouraging him, urging him to continue.

"I don't know what life has in store for her, but something tells me this is important to her future. We have to try, or nothing will be right. This feels bigger than just Illeina. It seems like it will affect the entire planet, and all of us here, too."

He wasn't lying. And if he was, it was only be-cause the silent whisper had told him to.

"Even if I wanted to teach you, Brother," Stiggens said, "I can't. It takes a considerable amount of energy to complete, and you don't have enough training, discipline, or experience to do what needs to be done."

As if he knew ze was going to speak, Stiggens' gaze caught Casey's, who already had zir mouth open. Ze closed it and waited for Stiggens to acknowledge zir.

"Teach me," ze said. "I can learn to do it."

"Again, you're offering to fight my battles," Adams grumbled. "You can't."

"It's fine," Casey argued. "I want to do it."

"Brother Adams, please leave us," Stiggens said.

"But—"

"Leave," Casey said. "We'll meet up later."

Reluctantly, Adams stood. Casey looked away, and despite watching zir as he walked to the exit and left, ze wouldn't meet his gaze.

Stiggens watched as Adams opened the door, gave them a long stare, and closed the door behind him. He waited until he was certain Adams was long gone.

"You've heard what this spell does, haven't you?" he asked.

"Yes," Casey replied.

"You won't survive. You'll be reduced to raw energy."

"I volunteered knowing that."

Stiggens took zir hands, and they shared a long look. Emotions flowed backward and forward between them. They both had been dead a long time, and Stiggens had a deep understanding of Casey's situation that Adams was unaware of. Casey could feel Stiggens's sadness at losing zir and could sense his wish for zir to tell Adams zir truth.

Casey had avoided it because it was uncomfortable to talk about, but it was definitely time. And Adams deserved to know.

CHAPTER 6

Fear that they wouldn't be allowed to return to Darkrealm weighed on Adams. He was gripped with indecision over whether to avoid or confront Casey, who surely thought he was wasting his time with this whole endeavor. But Adams knew as well as anyone that confronting one's problems is the best way to work through them—at least most of the time. There was something to be said for avoiding certain problems, like putting off work until the next day or walking around the Southern Training Grounds instead of risking your very existence by going through. But this wasn't one of those problems.

When Adams felt brave enough to look for Casey, ze was meditating in the safety of the Northern Training Grounds. He stood at the edge of the clearing, watching cautiously, eager to re-tether Illeina before it was too late—if it wasn't already. Was it hypocritical to want to rush Casey after taking his time coming to confront zir? Why yes, yes it was.

Casey sat completely still. A warm breeze caught Adams's shirt and shook the leaves of the surrounding trees, yet Casey remained stoic. Zir hair and clothes sat indifferent to the dynamic environment around them. He took a step forward, allowing his footstep to make a gentle sound to announce his presence. Casey's eyes slowly opened, and ze smiled when ze saw him.

"Come sit with me," ze said. "We need to talk about a few things."

Adams's reluctance, despite his best efforts, was plain on his face.

"Don't worry," ze assured him. "It won't take long."

He complied, sitting cross-legged on the ground in front of Casey and leaning forward, his elbows propped on his knees.

"Is everything okay?" he asked. "You seem . . . more somber than usual. Was learning the technique too difficult for you?"

"No," Casey replied, shaking zir head. "I feel confident about it." Ze took his hand. "But I need you to understand a few things before we go." Casey pushed some energy into Adams, just as Stiggens had done many times to show him new techniques. Ze used zir mind to talk to him, and Adams wondered if ze didn't want to be overheard. "Look at your back."

Adams didn't understand, but he turned his head to look. There, he saw something he'd never seen before. Giant streams of light curved and intertwined to form two large wings, each several times larger than him. The light glowed with a brilliance that almost blinded him. He reached his free hand back to try to touch them, but there was nothing tangible there.

Just giant wings made of light.

"What are they?" Adams asked.

Casey told him to focus, to communicate with his mind, and he repeated his question through his thoughts.

"It's something you'll learn later how to visualize. Now look around you at other angels. Tell me what you notice."

He used his power to search for other angels in the Training Grounds. The sight Casey was sharing with him revealed wings on every one. They came in many sizes, some far larger than his, some smaller. Some wings shone with a truly blinding intensity, while others shone dimly. He turned back to Casey, curious about zir wings, but there were none to be found. Ze turned to allow him to see zir back more clearly, but nothing was there.

"I don't understand," he thought to zir.

Ze squeezed his hand. "The wings you see are visual representations of our guilt. The size represents the size of the guilt, while the brightness represents the weight and seriousness of it. You feel incredibly guilty for your life, and the brightness tells me that you feel you've affected many people who you care about."

Adams couldn't argue with that. No wonder Casey had known so much about him when they first met.

Ze continued, "It's incredibly rude to ask someone about themselves or their lives, and that takes some getting used to. We learn this technique later in our training, after the curiosity to ask others about their lives subsides a little."

"But you . . ." He let his voice trail off, mostly because he didn't know what to ask or how to ask it.

"I have no wings. No guilt," Casey stated plainly. "And any angel who has gone through their training knows that."

"Is that why people act strangely around you?"

Casey sighed with a grin, as if relieved that Adams had indeed noticed, and nodded.

"But how is it possible?" he asked.

"I was a child, like Illeina. I'm the only one here like this. When I died, I was eleven and had no sense of regret yet."

"That's only a year older than Illeina. But how are you the only one?"

"Because other children either feel guilt by the time they die, or—and this happens most often—they choose to join with the Source or reincarnate."

"Why did you become an angel then, if no one else ever did?"

Casey's grin widened, and Adams got the distinct impression that grin was a patronizing one.

"I don't remember exactly," ze thought. "I just somehow knew I had to. My society was one where children with magic were conscripted into positions of power, doubly so for being born between sexes. I was very privileged as a child. When I died, I considered it my calling to help our planet through becoming an angel. And I guess, in my own way, I have made a difference."

"But. . ." Adams said, knowing there was another side to zir statement.

The smile drifted from Casey's lips, leaving a deep seriousness that Adams had rarely seen.

"But," ze continued with zir thoughts, "things here are difficult. Other angels are pleasant, but everyone understands that I'm different, even those who can't yet see our wings.

"It's hard for anyone to relate to me, I suppose. I haven't made many friends, and I get more pity than anything else. I even go by Casey instead of my living name to try to fit in better.

"I chose to work in the Archive because others seemed to be stressed at having me around. I've segregated myself for so long that—" Casey interrupted zirself. "Well, it doesn't matter now."

Casey's pulled Adams's other hand into zirs, and they clutched each other tightly as ze continued.

"Illeina's energy, what I could feel of it, seemed pure. She may be without guilt. If she becomes an angel, she'll be welcomed, but secluded. She'll always feel different somehow. She'll never feel right. I need you to understand that.

"There was a time when I thought I'd made the wrong decision. I thought about joining the Source or reincarnating. My every waking moment became consumed with a growing disdain for myself.

"And then I remembered Darkrealm.

"I learned of Whispers, about how they could change someone. It seemed a perfect solution. I would never have to bother or stress anyone again, yet I could

89

give back to the world by helping others fulfill their dreams. Whispers aren't inherently bad, you know. If kept under control, they're tools of success. And I was sure that I'd be able to make a difference there."

Adams didn't like where this story was going, and he had the tears in his eyes to prove it. Casey, on the other hand, was as solid and strong as a rock, continuing zir story seemingly untouched by how incredibly heart-breaking it was.

"So I went to Darkrealm," ze continued, "and I found Whispers, and I allowed them to touch me. But I didn't change. They were intrigued by me, but couldn't change me . . . or wouldn't change me. I just cried until I couldn't cry any longer, and then I sat and waited."

Casey stopped, almost as if the story ended there.

"And then? How did you get back here?" Adams asked.

The smile that crept back onto Casey's face was different this time, gentle and forlorn. "Brother Stiggens came for me. He had been following my progress, and an immortal had taken an interest in me, apparently. At their request, he came and brought me back.

"And here I am, still here somehow." Ze shrugged, one of those shrugs that you use when one thing leads to another but you can't recall which thing led to what.

Adams found such a shrug pretty out of scale with the tale ze had just shared, but who was he to judge?

"I'm sorry you had to go through all that," Adams thought to zir, putting his forehead to zirs. "But Illeina is going to live."

Casey threw zir arms around his neck and held their foreheads together.

"Adams, I've never felt this way before. In life, my family was my temple, and in death, the only family I've truly felt is with Brother Stiggens. But somehow, I know that I'm here, that I died and chose this path, all so I could meet you. All so I could help you. And all so I could help Illeina. I may not have a prophecy to tell me it's true, but I know it all the same."

Adams kissed zir forehead gently and held zir close. "I've felt it, too. We were destined to meet. And whatever immortal helped you, I think it's the same one who's helped me."

They shared a momentary smile.

"Adams, please tell me about your death," Casey said abruptly.

He jumped away, heart suddenly racing and perceived blood rushing to his face. "What?"

"I need to know what happened and why it happened. Everything." Although Adams wasn't thinking it in one coherent thought, Casey could obviously hear the question "why" circling around in his head. "The spell I must do works by sharing energy, syncing Illeina with my connection to Midrealm, in order to reconnect the two. If I don't know exactly what happened to her, I can't know what to expect when I start connecting our energy."

Casey paused.

"Also," ze said, with not one ounce of coyness or guilt, if you can believe it. "I've seen that you're troubled, and it seems that most of your guilt surrounds this one event. I really care for you, and so I want to know why."

Much of Adams's daily effort went toward trying not to recall this event. He was surprised ze would even ask, since this topic was typically taboo. But he couldn't find it in himself to deny zir this. After all, ze had just shared such intimate details about zir past.

So, he began with an explanation of the day he died.

It began the preceding evening, Illeina visiting his home and playing. It sometimes got late enough that he let her sleep at his place, and this had been one of those days.

Illeina had fallen asleep earlier than usual, probably worn out from all the gymnastics she'd been showing him. She'd learned tumbles and roundoffs in school and insisted on perfecting her technique. They had spent a few hours on that before he cooked dinner. By the time they finished eating, she was yawning.

He had called his sister, who suggested that Illeina stay the night.

"You can bring her home tomorrow morning," Amanda said. "Remember, I was planning on taking her shopping, so don't sleep in too late."

He agreed, and so Illeina snoozed against his back that night.

The next morning, he woke Illeina up early. They got ready, and he helped her onto his motorcycle. She seemed very awake, excitedly talking about what she and her mom were planning on buying.

He knew he was a little groggy. He promised himself he'd have a coffee once they got to his sister's home. With a yawn, he tightened his helmet and started the motorcycle.

His sister only lived a mile away. It had worked to their benefit, especially after Illeina was born, making it easy for them to see each other often. The roads along the way were residential, with few lights and mostly two- or four-way stops. It was a route he knew well, as he rode it practically every day.

There was one stop sign in particular where the crossroad traffic was free. He always wondered why the busier road that he was on was the one traffic-controlled instead of the cross-street. It annoyed him to no end. When he was by himself, sometimes he would glance both ways as he approached the street and coast through. There had only ever been a handful of times when he needed to stop for another vehicle passing the intersection in front of him.

It was different when Illeina was with him. Not once previously had he ever coasted through that stop sign with her riding, and he always took extra time to ensure it was safe to go through the intersection.

Perhaps it was that he was tired, or maybe it was the way Illeina had her head leaning against him that made him worry she was more tired than she seemed. Perhaps it was trying to understand her as she was talking loudly to him. Or maybe it was the sweet feeling of the morning dew brushing across his face. Whatever the reason, without looking, Adams completely forgot about the stop sign, not even slowing as he entered the intersection.

Chance would have it that a large van speeding down the crossroad collided with his bike and threw them both from it.

He died.

She didn't. Barely.

Peeking around the entertainment center, Adams confirmed that Illeina was where they left her. He looked around for a Whisper that could be controlling her, but didn't see one anywhere nearby. They checked the other side of the building, but again couldn't find a Whisper that could be controlling her.

"How far from her would a Whisper need to be to influence her?" he asked Casey.

"I would think pretty close, but I don't really know. Didn't you say the Whispers inside were right next to those they were influencing?"

Adams had said that. He'd wondered if that was how Whispers got their name, because they appeared to lean into their targets, as if whispering in their ear.

"Yes," he replied, "but that doesn't mean they need to be that close. Perhaps it's their preference. Or maybe they only need to be that close when they are in a large group of people."

"Do you see anything?" Casey asked.

He just shook his head.

It was nighttime, and the entertainment center was closed. All the energy and movement that had been here during their last visit were gone. Darkrealm itself didn't look any different. There was no night or day, no darkness or light. Yet Adams could clearly see Illeina.

She was bobbing her head back and forth, singing a song to herself as she always did when she was passing the time. He wondered what the Whisper could be trying to influence Illeina to do. She was an untethered spirit, after all. What could she do at this point?

It made sense to Adams that Whispers tried to control living people. They could be influenced to affect others, pursue goals, or commit crimes. As a wandering spirit, the Whispers could try to force Illeina away from her body. They might even have her meddle in the energy of others. Yet she was just sitting there, waiting.

Surely the Whispers were trying to draw her away from this place. Whatever goal they had for her, it seemed reasonable that she needed to get off that bench and follow them in order to reach it.

"We should check inside," Adams said. "The Whisper may be trying to draw her away and entice her with games."

"If that was the case, she'd be inside, wouldn't she?"

"She said she was waiting," he continued. "Illeina is stubborn. If she's waiting for something to happen, she won't leave."

"But she'd have to overpower the will of a Whisper," Casey rebutted. "She's a child, and that takes a lot more power than she could possibly have."

"Maybe, but let's check inside anyway."

They made their way into the building just as they had before—through the door. Adams hadn't made any major breakthroughs in the "walking through walls" department. The excited energy of the day was absent inside even more so than outside, and all that was left was the feeling they were being watched.

"There are Whispers here," Adams said in a hushed tone. "I can see them. Twenty, maybe more."

"This must be a good spot for them," Casey replied just as quietly. "Can you tell if one is controlling Illeina?"

Adams led the way, creeping among and between the Whispers, pulling Casey by the hand. He could see their emptiness, full of the darkest of blackness, yet seeming somewhat solid. They looked sleek, oily, and with a translucent shell, so you could see through to the darkness within. The sounds of the angels' footsteps echoed back at them from the walls, much louder than they should have, filling up the bare space where the people once were.

Adams looked behind them to see eyes. Lots of eyes. He stopped, clutching Casey's hand tightly. Glowing red and reflecting light that wasn't there, the eyes of every large shadow were on them.

Casey sensed his panic but didn't speak. Ze stuck close as he pulled zir away from where he was looking. Ze looked back and forth, seeing nothing yet knowing something was there. Suddenly, a Whisper took a step forward. It was more of a shift forward than a step, given how globby the Whispers were, but Adams thought he'd seen the ooze form a foot for a second there. This was just as disturbing as it sounds.

Casey jumped as ze saw a time-delayed movement.

"You were right, Adams. I saw one. How many did you say?" ze fussed in a whiny whisper.

"We'll be fine," he thought back.

"They almost got you last time. Adams, we should leave."

"Not without Illeina. Just trust me."

Abrupt jumps of darkness began filling the space behind them as Casey struggled not to look. Adams stopped hard. They were surrounded, Whispers creating a circle around them with no gaps to get away.

Adams could still feel that power within him, but he was unable to tap into it. He looked around for options, but the emptiness crept closer until it was almost touching him. Casey was clutching him hard, seeing the jerking movements of the Whispers rushing around them.

A rumble shook the ground beneath them. Its amplitude grew and diminished, making the air vibrate. The frequency of the wave increased until it seemed almost comprehensible.

"The . . . untouchable," it seemed to say in a seething voice, taking deep gasps between each word.

There was a long pause as the rumble pushed and pulled the air around them.

"And . . . the . . . stolen," the vague voice added.

Casey's nails digging into Adams's skin made it clear ze could hear this at least as well as he could. The voice was more in their heads than out loud, yet it matched with the vibrations that were moving through the room.

Adams wondered if he should reply, but chose to stay silent. The ground shook as the vibration grew more intense. The Whispers seemed to stretch upward and around them, creating a giant bubble of blackness, with terrifying red eyes almost seeming like stars swirling past.

He reached for his latent power, grasping at it. It was there but out of reach, like the last penny in the piggy bank. Yet he reached even harder.

Illeina appeared before them, dirty with mud and blood.

"It's too late, you know," she said. "You really should leave while you still can."

"No," Adams said. "It's not real."

He looked to Casey, whose eyes were large as ze stared at the little girl.

"Casey, it's not real," he assured zir.

"I know," ze said, voice cracking.

"It's an untouchable," Illeina continued, pointing at Casey with a wry smile. "It wasn't even supposed to be allowed in Highrealm."

"Don't listen," Adams yelled.

"Its heritage demanded reincarnation!"

Illeina's doppelganger laughed heartily, and when it closed and opened its eyes, they were a bright red, beaming back at the angels like lasers.

"You denied your people by crossing into High-realm."

Adams stole another glance at Casey. Tears were in zir eyes.

"I want to leave," Casey cried. "I want to go back to Highrealm. Now."

Suddenly, Illeina was inches away from them, looking up. She reached her arm up to grab Casey, who yelped. Adams grabbed the pretend child's wrist.

"You'll be one of us," Illeina said to Adams.

He shook as he desperately clutched her tiny, powerful arm. The power he needed was right there. Why couldn't he grasp it?

"Once this abomination is gone, we'll have you **and** your connection to Highrealm."

"You'll have nothing," Adams said.

Illeina grabbed him with her other arm. She pushed him down, forcing him onto his knees. All he needed was a little more time, a little more energy, a little more power.

He had none of it.

"It's speaking to you even now, yet you can't hear because you don't listen. **We** will listen."

Listen.

He needed to listen.

Beneath the pounding vibration of the Whispers was a silence, a silence that Adams recognized but could barely understand. This silence had spoken to him many times, perhaps even more often than he realized. It spoke without words.

It spoke with silence.

What the Whispers were talking about, this connection to Highrealm they craved, was it this silence?

He resigned himself to stop reaching for the power from before, instead focusing his energy on that silent voice. He allowed the Whisper to throw him to the ground. He ignored Casey's scream. His mind drifted into the void where the silent voice waited.

It spoke with gentleness and without urgency, and he finally understood.

"I see you have found me. You have questions. I know. I have answers, yet not necessarily to the questions you have been asking. You must listen now. All will become clear. Time is irrelevant, so do not be distressed. I will explain to you what you need to know to fulfill your destiny, so you must stay in this state until I am finished. I see you understand.

"You understand. I brought your friend, now it goes by Casey, to Highrealm after it died. It served a purpose of reincarnation for its people. Each cycle of its death and rebirth brought them renewed knowledge. They used this knowledge to flourish. They built cities, formed a large community, cured disease, built technology, and kept balance with Terra, your Earth in Midrealm. Its purpose in all of this was vast, and its people loved it. I took it away from them, brought it to Highrealm, to serve my purpose. Its people have long since disappeared, and their bones lie at the bottom of the ocean as sand.

"As sand. Casey's purpose was to prepare for something grander, something which I will bring to you, to Terra, to Midrealm. I know it found this difficult, knowing it should be alive and yet being unable to protect those it loved, but it was necessary. I was preparing it for you, and for what is beyond you. You see, this something that is larger and greater—this gift I will bring to Midrealm—it comes later, after you. Yet you are an integral part of its creation and growth.

"Creation and growth. You were meant to leave Terra through death. You were meant to become an angel. It is not explicit in prophecy, but woven into the margins. I brought you Casey. I brought you the proper training. I brought the Whispers to you, to change you. I did it so you could prepare. You needed to be ready for this day and beyond. And you are. You have learned all you need to know, and you must succeed here.

"You must succeed here. I brought the Whispers to Illeina. They changed her, too. They've made her special, as I need her to be special, just as Casey is special. It all serves a grander purpose that you and it and others will all be a part of. I brought it to this place; I brought you to this place; I brought Illeina to this place. So you must succeed.

"Hear me, and succeed. See the staff just before your eyes. I have placed it there, brought it close enough so that you can see it. Come closer, in your mind, and feel the warmth of it surrounding you. It is there inside you, waiting for you to grasp it. Accept its glow, come closer still, move deeper into your mind. It is there now, just before you, just within your grasp. Accept its power, allow it to do its will. Grasp it and succeed.

"Grasp it and succeed."

CHAPTER 7

When Adams opened his eyes, he was no longer on the ground. He was standing, holding a Whisper who had taken Illeina's image. Without any of the effort he had been exerting before, his power grew. His skin emanated light, which reached its tendrils out to every Whisper in the bubble surrounding them.

The Whisper before him lost its hold on the image of a child and began to retreat. He grasped it and pulled it toward him, pushing disruption into it. The disruption spread through it, cracking first its sticky shell and then ripping through its very essence. Shattered pieces flew in every direction, caught by fellow Whispers and integrated into themselves. Glowing eyes faded, and black bodies receded. They formed a path, a goopy tunnel for them to travel through, still and obedient.

He was in control.

Adams looked down to see Casey at his side. He put a hand out, and ze used it to stand up.

"You figured it out, it seems," ze said. "Took you long enough."

"And I didn't even have to hit you," he replied.

Casey gave him a small smack on the shoulder before grabbing his arm.

"Let's go. Please," ze urged, and they started their way down the Whispers' path.

The path opened to outside, where Illeina was sitting at the same bench where she had been waiting all this time. She was tapping her feet to some internal song, eyes locked on the parking lot. Adams stepped toward her cautiously. The movement caught her eye, and she turned to look at him.

"Illeina?" he said gently.

She retracted into herself a little. Clearly, she still viewed him as a stranger.

"Do you know me?" she asked.

He smiled gently and knelt at the other end of the bench, careful not to intrude on her personal space.

"What are you doing here?" he asked.

"I'm waiting for someone."

"Who?"

She paused a moment. She took her long hair in her hands and stroked it as she thought.

"I'm not sure. But I know I have to tell someone something. It's very important. And I'm supposed to wait here until I can see them so I can tell them. So I'm here."

"Do you know where you are?"

She gave him a strange look and pointed up at the sign. "At the arcade," she said as if he was an idiot.

And maybe she was a little bit right.

"Are you waiting for your family?" Casey spoke up. Illeina looked at zir but didn't answer, so Casey continued. "Because we know where your family is. They're at the hospital still, where you came here from. And they're waiting for you. They miss you very much and want you to come home to them. I'm sure the person you're waiting for is there with them, waiting to hear what you have to say."

Illeina's eyes were locked on Casey's. "I've been waiting here for a very, very long time."

Casey walked around Adams and sat next to her. Ze leaned forward so ze was at Illeina's eye level.

"I know. You've been a good girl. But you've been waiting in the wrong place."

"But he told me he'd be here."

"Who?"

"I don't know."

The lump in Adams's throat was silencing him, but he swallowed it back. He moved closer and reached out. When she didn't move away, he placed a hand on hers.

"You were supposed to come here together with him," he said.

Illeina looked from one of them to the other. Her look was one of almost recognition.

"Do you know me? Do you know where I can find him?" she asked.

"He's at the hospital, waiting for you," he replied, eyes watering. "I can't offer you any proof, but we can take you there."

"What do I have to do?" she asked.

"You don't have to do anything you don't want to. We'll wait until you're ready."

He stood and put his hand out for her to take. She thought for a long moment. She kicked her feet out and looked around. As if trying to see how long they'd really wait, she took one finger and rolled her hospital bracelet around with it.

Then, abruptly, she stood.

"I'm ready," she said plainly.

She wobbled as she tried to take a step forward. Throwing her arms out to her sides, she flung her foot out in front of her as if she didn't have control. As she lost her balance, Adams caught her and put her back upright.

"What's wrong?" he asked.

"She's just weak," Casey replied.

"Illeina, would you like me to carry you?"

She nodded and climbed onto his back when he bent down. He pulled her up and put an arm around each of her legs. She lay her head on his shoulder.

"Don't worry. Everything's going to be fine," he promised.

It wasn't long after they started walking that Illeina started asking questions. She wanted to know how they knew her, where they had come from, how far they were walking, everything. They danced around the answers, telling her what they could while trying not to confuse her. Adams couldn't help the overwhelming happiness he was feeling.

This little girl had been the light of his life. The moment she was born, he had fallen in love with her little nose, her bright eyes full of wonder, and even her loud cry. It was as if she was his own child, even as his sister and her husband coddled their new infant. He still remembered Amanda looking up at him, calling him over, and introducing her to him.

He was never the same after that.

It wasn't that Illeina's birth changed his life. He had a job he loved and a sister he spent as much time with as possible. His life before Illeina's birth wasn't too removed from his life after. But he felt a deep connection with her, a sense of fulfillment, as if they were meant to be together, to work together on some larger scale.

When he had told Amanda this, she thought it was the sweetest thing she had ever heard. She encouraged him to spend time with his niece, but she also expressed that he may be ready to settle down. She regularly asked him about his love life. He went on the occasional date and had been intimate with several people: men, women, and some who lay beyond those simple ideas. These brief relationships brought him happiness, and none ended on a bad note. Yet, he never felt tied to anyone. Amanda often offered to set him up with friends or friends of friends, and he always responded with a light chuckle and a "no, thank you."

Thinking back on this, he sighed at how selfish he'd been. All Amanda had ever wanted was a big family, and while her husband's family welcomed her lovingly, he knew that wasn't enough. As this little girl clung to his shoulders, he felt a welcome sense of relief that he could finally give Amanda something back, after all that had been taken from her.

His mind wandered back to the words that had washed over him, that had helped him reach his power. Something told him he shouldn't tell anyone about what happened. He somehow knew this experience was special, intimate, and meant for him alone.

However, what he'd heard weighed on him. Somehow, he could remember every word as if it was sitting right in front of him. He went over it many times in his head, touching every nuance of its meaning. He was part of some plan, some "grander" plan. Some entity had changed Casey's future, had changed his future, was changing Illeina's future. The goal of this being was vague, perhaps even beyond his comprehension. Yet three lives from Earth had been touched and connected.

He couldn't help but wonder about the identity of that silent voice. It was obviously no Midrealm creature, as how would it be able to reach him in the Realm of the Angels or Darkrealm? It couldn't be a Whisper, as they held no connection to Highrealm. It was possible it was an angel, though it would have to be a more powerful angel than any he had met.

The only option that made sense was that this was an entity from the area of Highrealm closer to the Source, an immortal. This immortal had brought Casey to the angelic realm, had influenced the High Council to have Stiggens train Adams, had urged him to act to save Illeina, had put a target on him for the Whispers, had helped Illeina survive in Darkrealm longer than she should have, and likely so many other things that he thought it best to stop trying to list them. He wondered if he should feel like a pawn on a complex chess board too large for him to see from his small square, but he couldn't bring himself to feel that way. In fact, it all seemed right. Each act alone made no sense, but together, somehow, it did.

Not that he could comprehend the purpose behind it all. But then, he wasn't some super powerful immortal being close to the Source, was he? How could a measly little angel like him hope to understand?

He looked over at Casey, who was trying to determine how much his niece remembered about her life and her time in Darkrealm. He was overwhelmed with a sense of adoration at Casey's story. How many lifetimes had ze lived? How many deaths had ze endured? Ze retained an amazing optimism about zir existence, despite everything that had happened. He wondered how ze could have become an angel, knowing that ze had been pulled from zir people. His friend was one of the strongest people he'd ever met. A loving warmth filled him, an intense pride just to know zir.

Illeina began tugging backwards on his neck. He stopped.

"I know that place," she exclaimed, pointing at the hospital in the distance.

"You recognize it?" Casey asked.

"Yes. Yes, I think so," Illeina replied. "I think I've been there."

"That's where we're going," Adams said.

"And my family is there?"

"That's right."

She began kicking her legs and crying out happily for them to hurry. This made it difficult to hold onto her, but she also refused to get down and walk. Luckily, it wasn't long before they were inside the lobby.

"Where are they?" she asked as soon as they stepped in the door.

"The reports gave the room number," Casey paused and looked up, trying to remember.

"Room 1339," Adams said.

Casey gave him a patronizing pat on the arm, as if to tell him how silly he looked for remembering that.

He took in the clamor around him. There were many people rushing this way and that, the characteristic wispiness following them as it always did in Darkrealm. Doctors, patients, friends, families, all completely ignorant to this second level of their existence. Spotted around were Whispers, hovering over or sitting next to or following people around the room.

He remembered Casey's assertion that they weren't innately evil. It seemed to him they longed for the corporeal, wished to be among the living, just as he wanted for Illeina. In that moment, he found some peace with the creatures, feeling he could understand in some small way why they influenced those in Midrealm. Soon, he would reunite his niece with his family there. How fulfilling that would be, and how gratifying it must be for the Whispers to achieve their wishes in someone!

"Not long now," he said gently to Casey.

Ze smiled and led the way with confidence.

Their footsteps were all too quiet as they traveled down the halls toward the stairs. There should have been intercom calls, footsteps, and conversations, but the space seemed bare and empty. Just as their footsteps had reverberated too much at the entertainment center, so now did their footsteps echo too little. He shook his head gently, trying not to think of all the reasons why this realm could change the dynamics so much.

A small voice reached out from his back. "I think I had two daddies," Illeina said quietly. "And a mommy."

"Yeah?" Adams asked.

"I think so. I really loved them. All of them."

"They love you, too, Illeina."

"Yeah, I think they did." She nuzzled her face into the back of his neck. "Thank you for bringing me to them. Maybe I would have been stuck waiting there forever if it weren't for you and Casey. I love you both, too."

Adams smiled, ignoring the pull of guilt that reminded him he was the reason she was untethered in Darkrealm to begin with.

"Will you stay with me a while? Even after I find my family?" Illeina asked.

"Sure," Adams said.

"For a while," Casey agreed.

Illeina seemed shy as they approached room 1339. She asked to be let down, and Adams allowed her to hold his arm for balance. She wavered. Casey held out a hand, and Illeina took it. She peeked into the room, and then pulled back, hiding in case someone saw her.

"What's wrong?" Casey asked.

"He's not there," Illeina said.

"Who?"

"My daddy. One of my daddies. The one I needed to tell something to."

Casey and Adams shared a long gaze as Illeina's eyes teared up and her lip began to quiver.

"Illeina, I saw your Mommy in there and your Daddy. I'm sure the one you're looking for is nearby," Casey said, kneeling next to her.

"What if he forgot about me," Illeina said.

Casey pulled her into a hug and patted her back. "No, no, no. That's impossible. He loves you very much, and he'll be here. He's just waiting for you to wake up. That's all."

"Wake up?"

"That little girl on the bed is you. You've been sleeping a very long time, so long that you can't remember so well. We're your guardian angels and are going to help you wake up so you can be with your family again. Do you understand?"

"I'm sleeping?" Illeina asked.

"That's right."

"So, this is a dream?"

"It's similar to a dream," Casey explained. "Except it's not a dream. We're really here, helping you. But even though we're really here, you're asleep."

"Like . . . astral atection?"

"Astral projection," Adams corrected, and she looked up at him. "That's right, Illeina. Just like astral projection."

"And you're going to help me stop astral protection? Is it going to hurt?"

"It won't hurt you one teeny, tiny bit," Casey insisted. "But you'll remember all sorts of things all at once, and you may feel a little sad."

Illeina gave them both long looks, back and forth, over and over. She gripped their hands lovingly. Finally, she nodded, and pushed forward into the hospital room, pulling them behind her.

The lump returned to Adams's throat when he saw that his sister and her husband really were there at the hospital, almost as if they knew she was about to wake up. They were talking, but he couldn't make out what they were saying. Casey instructed Illeina to stand next to her body and stay calm, yet that sound, too, seemed to disappear.

His mind drifted back to Illeina's first day of school.

She had insisted he be there to drop her off, so Amanda had begged him to go into work late that day. His coworkers thought it was strange, to be sure, that he needed to be late in order to take his niece to her first day of school. But they had all been working together long enough to know Illeina had him wrapped around her tiny finger.

When the day came, he met them all at their house. Illeina had made goodbye cards for each of them out of construction paper and had haphazardly written "BYE" on each. He knew Amanda had helped her since Illeina wasn't able to write yet. Illeina did her best to appear resolute in her mission, and he remembered being unsure if she understood she'd be returning home that afternoon. Despite her brave face, he could tell from the way she chewed on her lip that she was afraid.

He rode her to school on his bike at her request, with Mom and Dad right behind them. Adams had expected a long goodbye once they got there, but instead, she gave them each a hug and a kiss, straightened her bag, and gave a convincing smile. Then she was gone.

That strong smile was on her face now, and he found Casey and Illeina a fitting pair. Casey looked down at Illeina's body and touched her forehead gently. Then ze came over to Adams. Ze put zir arms around his neck and pulled him close into a hug.

"Thank you," ze said simply.

"What are you saying? I should be thanking you, for everything," he replied.

"You should know that you've done just as much for me." Ze smiled and gripped him tightly again.

He put a hand on zir head and pulled it tightly against him. He wasn't sure he would ever find the words or actions to express his gratitude, but he could show appreciation for having Casey in his life . . . his afterlife.

"Of course," he said.

114

Ze reluctantly pulled away. "I should get started."

Adams let go, too, and Casey took zir place again at Illeina's side. Ze put zir arms out and held them above Illeina's body. As ze took a deep breath in and out, ze closed zir eyes.

"Once I begin, there is no stopping," ze said, "so don't even consider it an option."

"What do you mean? What are you talking about?"

Adams received no response, except for a surge of energy pushing from zir as ze began to mutter a spell under zir breath.

A bright light exploded from within Casey, encasing the surrounding area in pure whiteness, as white as the space where he had first met Stiggens and decided to become an angel. Despite having to squint his eyes against the glaring light, Adams had no trouble seeing zir.

The air changed. He wasn't sure exactly how, but he could tell that the distance between Midrealm and Darkrealm was decreasing. It was as if Casey was creating a sinkhole, allowing this portion of Darkrealm to level off with Midrealm, which sat slightly below it. He could also sense a change with his power. His power was different in Darkrealm, and he could feel the two types mixing. Casey seemed to be collapsing this portion of Darkrealm into Midrealm.

The air pulsed, followed by the floor beneath him. They were asynchronous, making him dizzy. Illeina seemed astounded but unbothered by the change, while he could just make out Amanda and her husband, sitting in their chairs and talking gently. Although their voices had been strange and muffled in Darkrealm, it was becoming clearer as the space collided.

"I know they said there was nothing left they could do," Amanda said, "but it just seems wrong."

"This is our second opinion," her husband replied. "We could get a third, but I don't know if it will do us any good. How long are we going to let her lay there and suffer before we let her go?"

"It's not like she's dead. She's right there."

"Honey, I'd never tell you that we have to pull the plug. I don't want to lose her any more than you do. But we do need to decide how long we are willing to wait. We don't have unlimited funds, and every day she stays in this condition, the odds of her coming out of it goes down."

"I know." She took a deep breath and a long look at her young daughter. "You're right. I've avoided it long enough. It's time to let her go."

Her husband took her in his arms, tears coming to his eyes.

"Let's spend this one last night with her, and then we'll talk to the doctor in the morning."

CHAPTER 8

The energy of the room changed abruptly, and a sense of dread and fear overcame Adams. Something was wrong with this whole process. He'd been so distracted, he'd almost missed it. His stomach dropped. This wasn't right.

Casey's light was fading. Illeina's Darkrealm soul was glowing now, and tendrils of light were reaching out from her all over the room, as if searching for her body. Casey was weakening, zir legs were shaking, and zir form was thinning.

"Casey, what's happening?" Adams shouted.

Ze struggled to open zir eyes and look at him.

"What have you done?" he asked. He tried to take a step toward zir, but an invisible force pushed against him.

"It'll all be worth it," Casey replied.

"What's happening?" he repeated.

117

"I've existed a long time, Adams. And now, I can finally give back to the world. This is what I was meant for. It's what I've always been meant to do."

"Casey, no!"

"It's fine," ze assured him.

He pulled all his power together and forced himself forward, throwing his arms around what was left of zir shoulders.

Ze said, "My connection to Midrealm will align Illeina's self with her body. She'll live again. Everything will be as it should be."

"Why didn't you tell me you were going to do this?" Adams cried.

"I knew you wouldn't let me, of course," ze said with a patronizing laugh. "I meant everything I said about my feelings, okay?"

"Me, too, Casey. And everything I thought."

Ze nodded. As if disintegrating right in front of him, Casey's form began to dissipate.

"Goodbye, my dearest friend," ze thought softly to him.

Zir last particle drifted away.

The room seemed empty and dead. He turned back to Illeina, wiping the tears from his eyes while new ones formed in their place. Her eyes were wide and sparkling as she looked up at him.

"Uncle?" she asked. "Why are you here like this?"

"You remember me?" he asked.

The tendrils of light were still swooping this way and that, interrogating every inch of space in the room, trying desperately to find her body and connect them once again.

"I was waiting for you, Uncle. I had something to tell you."

"I'm sorry it took me so long to find you, baby."

"It's fine," she said with a smile. "But you . . . does this mean you're dead?" He nodded, and her face saddened. "And now Casey has risked everything for me."

"Because we all love you."

He could hardly believe it when Illeina nodded as if she understood. He suddenly realized that the light tendrils were fading away, so quickly that by the time he looked around to assess their strength, they were gone.

"What? No!" he yelled, tears forming. "It has to work! There has to be something we can do. I'll get Stiggens, and he can teach me, or try again. Maybe we can salvage what Casey did."

Illeina walked around her body and took her uncle's hands in hers. She looked up at him as he rambled on, grasping for solutions that weren't there.

"It's important, the thing I needed to tell you," she said.

He finally looked down to meet her gaze, tears escaping down his cheeks.

"You've always taken care of me, Uncle. Always. And I knew as soon as you found out I was hurt, you'd blame yourself. I was waiting for you because I needed to tell you. Things are okay how they are. I know you think you have to save me, just like you've always been there to save me."

This couldn't be happening, he said to himself. He couldn't have failed her.

"Uncle, you don't need to save me," she said, pulling him out of his "what if"s and "maybe"s and "I wish"es.

Illeina sounded strange, grown up, almost as if she was already starting to receive the angelic knowledge. Tears he had been failing to hold back streamed down his face as he realized his options were gone. This was inevitable.

"I wanted this to work," she continued, "but it didn't. Now that I know I can't go back to them, I'm at peace with that." She squeezed his hands. "They've been suffering, and you've been suffering. You all have suffered for my sake. I think it'd be better if I didn't just lay in that bed any longer. I think it would be better to let everyone move on."

He dropped down to his knees and hugged her close. She squeezed him tightly, even though her little arms could barely wrap all the way around him.

"Uncle." She waited for him to pull away before she continued. "I understand that I have a choice. A choice about staying wherever I am now, to keep my body alive, and a choice about afterwards. I really do think it's best." She gave him a kiss on the cheek. "I have to go. If I move farther from my body, it will die. We'll see each other soon."

His mind went back to Casey's experience in the Realm of the Angels. Zir loneliness and fears, and zir insistence that Illeina not endure those same struggles.

However, seeing her here in front of him, he couldn't bring himself to speak.

The words of the silent voice were clear in his mind, telling him that Illeina's future remained unfixed. Despite her death, she was still important, and the plans that had been set into motion were still fulfilling themselves as they were meant to. When he inquired in thought as to whether her death was part of the plan, the answer eluded him.

With an encouraging smile from Illeina, he stood. He finally understood what he needed to do. There was nothing left to be done here, but he still needed answers.

"Yes," he whispered. "I'll see you soon. It's a promise."

He kissed her nose and hurried out of the room.

Illeina turned to her parents and moved toward them. She apologized for leaving them, told them how much she loved them, and told them not to worry about her.

"I'll be with Uncle forever now. So, I'll be okay. And someday, we'll be able to see each other again, too, I hope."

She only took one more look at her body. Then, she left.

The night dragged on in that Midrealm hospital room.

Murmurs from the hallway didn't distract Illeina's parents from their quiet contemplation. As the sun rose, they stood over her body, held her hands tenderly, and lay warm kisses on her cheeks and lips and forehead. They poured their love into her for the last time.

And as they said goodbye, her monitor alarmed. A long trailing beep penetrated the air, and they held each other close with fear and regret and a terrible hollowness that would remain with them for the rest of their lives, even as they rebuilt them.

Something in the energy of the Realm of the Angels told Adams that Illeina's life was over, that a new chapter had begun. He was sure she would be arriving soon, and he'd be able to share with her everything he had built here. He promised himself she would never feel strange, never feel lonely, never feel isolated. Part of him was screaming to be there for her when she arrived, but he knew that some competent and not emotionally drained angel was assigned to her intake.

He had more pressing needs.

As he walked, the Realm changed around him. He adjusted his perception to see the beautiful night sky Casey had been so comforted by, to feel grass under his bare feet wherever he stepped, to hear the gentle trickling of the streams that flowed under and all around the Realm. It was as if Casey was right here with him, and it gave him comfort—even if it was only slight.

Something in him begged for answers, and he knew there was only one place he would find them. There was one being who had forced Casey to become an angel, who had brought them together, who had sent Stiggens to train him. This same being had allowed him to be influenced and molded by the Whispers in Darkrealm, had kept Illeina alive by changing her with the Whispers' power, and had somehow destined her for death. This same being was responsible for pushing Illeina to become an angel, and yet he had no understanding of why.

The Southern Training Grounds, as Casey had described them, were impenetrable by angels. He stood outside the massive entrance and could feel the power within. Within these walls lay the gates to the area of Highrealm that was closer to the Source. Beyond looked to be a vast desert, winds blowing dust into spiraling cyclones. Farther in the distance, he thought he could make out an oasis of trees. The Training Grounds seemed to breathe as if they were alive, and they beckoned him inside.

He took a deep breath and stepped over the threshold.

He didn't disappear. The silent voice had told him he was special, that he could survive the Training Grounds. And so it was.

The air itself felt dense within the walls, but he pushed forward, toward the trees that became more and more defined as he trod through the dirt. His powers were enhanced here, he could tell. Just as powers were enhanced in the Northern Training Grounds, here they were at his fingertips, as if begging to be used, but far more powerful than he'd ever felt. The power threatened to tear his spirit apart, and he fought against his terror. He focused his mind, working diligently to control the power with every step forward he took.

The dirt transitioned into sand as his surroundings transformed into a desert landscape. Every grain of sand seemed to have a purpose, and the distant trees waved in a strange, unnatural wind as he neared them, calling him ever closer.

By the time he stepped into the brush under the trees, his control was complete. Somehow, he had gained power strong enough to enter this place. And he sure wasn't going to question such a gift. The act of walking through the grounds had taught him how to control the new level of ability he had been granted.

He was drawn into the depths of the trees, which hid a deep forest. The humidity was suffocating and the ground was thick with detritus, yet he pushed onward until he reached its far edge.

Beyond lay a rocky terrain that reached up into the sky. Though he hadn't seen a mountain when he entered the Training Grounds, it didn't dissuade him. He reaffirmed his personal mission for answers and began the jagged ascent. Climbing, stepping, slipping, and pulling himself along, he forced his way up length by length. He refused to look up, lest he delude himself into believing that his climb was near its end. Though difficult, the path had been laid out for him, pulling his eyes down to it as if daring him to look away.

Finally, there was no more up, no more trail, no more mountains, no more rocks. Just white, as if the world ended in front of him in a blaze of Light. The wind that had been pushing him on now pushed back against him, hard enough that he had to place a foot behind him to keep his balance. He put an arm up in front of his face and thrust himself forward. Each step brought him closer to the Light, while each step also brought a stronger and stronger force working to push him back.

His feet slipped from under him, and he fell to the ground. He tried to push himself up, but the force weighed down on him, holding him against the nothingness beneath.

His confidence wavered. Was this the end? Would he never know why Casey had to disappear? Would he never know what was in store for Earth, even after all he'd been through? Would he never understand how he was meant to use these new powers, powers which seemed excessive, even for an angel?

Just as he questioned himself, the silent voice seemed to echo his doubts back at him.

"No!" he cried out. "I'm ready!"

The overwhelming force stopped abruptly. When he lifted his gaze, a black gate lay before him. It seemed to be made of a glittering ebony and detailed in sparkling gold, and it stood in stark contrast against the white emptiness. Full of remorse, full of guilt, but also full of resolve, he pushed himself up to his feet and stepped forward. Without hesitation, he touched the gate. It opened, and Adams stepped through.

His guilt washed away, his remorse was alleviated, and his future began.

And damn, it felt good.

THANK YOU

Thank you for reading *Those Without Wings*.

Your support means the world to me. Please consider leaving a review of this book on retailer websites or on review sites such as Goodreads or Storygraph. I'm a small indie author, so every review will help other readers find my work, even if it only contains a couple sentences.

Looking for more? See the next page for ways to connect with me!

You can find me on social media as gaiusjaugustus.

Connect With Gaius

Become part of the magic at my Magician's Club HQ. Join for free to get access to exclusive stories, regular updates, and behind-the-scenes peeks. Or upgrade to a premium plan for early access and additional rewards. New episodes are released regularly!

Sign up for the MCHQ at
https://gaiusjaugustus.com/mchq/

Get 20% off premium plans with the code TWW25.

Want less frequent updates of my ongoings? Sign up for my newsletter at
https://gaiusjaugustus.com/signup/

MORE FROM GAIUS

MANIFESTATION OF PROPHECY

Though they come from two vastly different realms, Maliah and Jarith are tied together by a prophecy that promises ascension after death. However, fate has a mischievous sense of humor, as Maliah must reluctantly embrace magical abilities she's afraid she can't control, while Jarith is burdened with an unthinkable task: murdering Maliah's mother.

Neither Maliah nor Jarith are keen to fulfill this prophecy. That is, until a formidable magician threatens their very existence, determined to halt the prophecy in its tracks. The weight of the world rests upon their shoulders, but is the future truly set in stone? In this quirky fantasy, the path set by destiny proves to be anything but straightforward.

Learn more at https://gjabooks.com/mani

The Magician and the Mechanical Doll, Tales of a Vernian Youth Volume 1

Octavian, a promising graduate student of magic, is about to have his dreams shattered. As he activates his magical robot, Replika, the duo finds themselves thrust into an alternate reality of stuck doors and steam-powered tech. Little did Octavian know that his enigmatic research advisor, Teacher, held the technology to traverse realities! Octavian and Replika embark on a quest to uncover Teacher's hidden secrets and find their way back home.

Get ready for a whimsical, magic-filled adventure that spans time and space, transporting our travelers to fantastical destinations. Are you ready to traverse the boundaries of our reality? Don't miss out on this epic journey!

Learn more at https://gjabooks.com/ToVY

ABOUT THE AUTHOR

Gaius (they/them) is a transgender, queer, disabled author who writes magical stories with diverse characters. In their work, they aim to convey immersive plots with unique worlds and irreverent humor. They have a distinctive background, going to university for film & television before later returning to school to complete a PhD in Cancer Biology. This colors their storytelling as they blur the boundaries of dichotomies such as magic & science, drama & humor, and good & evil.

Learn more about Gaius at gaiusjaugustus.com

www.ingramcontent.com/pod-product-compliance
Lightning Source LLC
Chambersburg PA
CBHW050413110726
47899CB00008B/2701